BRAZEN

M. MALONE

NANA MALONE

BRAZEN

CHAPTER ONE

Oskar

"Are you sure you want to handle it like this?"

I grinned at my partner. "Sure. Come on, kid, why not?"

Matthias Weller shook his head at me. "Maybe because Gemma has been asking why every time I go out with you, I come back with blood on my clothes."

I rolled my eyes. "That thing with the prince. You didn't come back with blood on your clothes because of me. It turned out Prince Lucas was kind of a handful."

Matthias nodded and considered that one. "True. All I'm

saying is maybe a private meeting would have been a good idea."

I grinned. "Nope. It's better that it's all out on the table, and then no one has any time to make up lies and come up with excuses and reasons. This is for the best."

The kid just shook his head. I would have sworn, since he got engaged, he'd been extra careful. Noah had kept him away from a lot of the violence before, but recently he'd mellowed, which was fine by me. It was good to see the kid a lot less stabby. He no longer seemed to have a death wish, or rather a kill wish. Rafe and the new kid, Tyse, rounded out the crew at the Stanley Co. meeting.

The new kid was untested, so he'd be shadowing one of the best of us for at least another few months.

Rafe cracked his neck. "If you two are done discussing china patterns, can we get this show on the road?"

Tyse said nothing, just shrugged, ready and willing as always.

Benson Grove, the CEO of Stanley Co., had called Blake Security because he was getting death threats. Two point five million had vanished off the books. And he swore up and down he hadn't taken it.

From what I'd seen of the company books, he hadn't. The problem was someone had tried to kill him over it. That was when he'd called us. The good news was I knew the truth about who *had* taken the money. The bad news, for him, was that the truth was going to hurt.

When we walked in, Benson stood up. "Mueller." He greeted me with a nod. He nodded at the others, but I was his main point of contact. The CFO stood as well, as did the VP and a couple of their executives.

I admit, at the beginning, I hadn't bothered learning their names. If they didn't show up in my financial investigation, I really didn't care.

When everyone sat, I stayed standing. I had my presentation all ready. I almost looked profesh. Little did these guys know that I'd been born a thief, had grown up a thief, and until recently had I turned into, well, *not* a thief. There once was a time when it came to hiding money, I was your guy. I could find every single loophole so that rich assholes didn't have to pay any taxes.

I also had a knack for making money too. Some of the less than savory people I used to work with called me Midas. I was the expert at money. Just like when it came to hacking, Matthias was the best there was.

"Mr. Grove, I hope you've been happy with the work that Blake Security has done for you so far."

Benson nodded. "Yeah, it's been fine. Great. I hardly knew you guys were here most of the time, but then every time I'd so much as sneeze, one of you would appear out of the shadows. It's eerie, but good work."

I gave him a wan smile. We didn't need a pat on the back; we knew how good we were. Frankly, if he'd noticed Tyse as his security detail, I'd be all over Noah to fire the kid. "Great, great. Well, the good news is you will no longer need us."

Everyone looked around.

"I know. Surprising. But it's completely unnecessary. No one is going to kill you. No one was ever trying to kill you. Someone just wanted you scared enough to change all the security protocols."

Benson frowned. "I don't understand."

This was my favorite part. Where I got to shine. "Well, it's pretty complicated, but it has to do with the access codes you use for your upper level accounts. The person who stole from you only took two million to see if they could get you to change your protocols. And when you did, thanks to some hacker friends of theirs, they were able to quietly siphon off another fifteen million that you wouldn't have noticed for at least another few months."

Benson stood. "What the hell are you saying?"

I had to try not to be so smug. No one liked a showoff. Didn't matter how awesome I was. I flipped on the projector, showing a whole bunch of numbers, graphs, and spreadsheets. I knew to most people these were boring, but to me this shit was almost as good as an orgasm. *Almost.* It didn't make sense, really, the way the numbers spoke to me, considering I was so affable. They made the most sense to me than people. And while I didn't generally like to lie, if I *needed* to lie, the numbers could help me.

I pointed at the projector screen. "Do you see that right there?" I pointed to a highlighted line. Then I scrolled the pointer down to another highlighted line and repeated the process for about five records. Finally, I pointed at the account number, matching the transactions. "That account number right there is at Allied Financial Bank."

Benson's brows rose. "I don't know that bank."

I shook my head. "You're not expected to."

"Okay, I don't understand."

I shrugged. "Well, Allied Financial is in the Caymans. They're not supposed to tell you who their clients are. And in some cases, they don't even know. But thanks to my boy Matthias—" I clapped Matthias on the shoulder and he lifted a brow. Sometimes I forgot about the whole *it's still not a good idea to touch him unexpectedly* thing, but this time I didn't even see any hint of the monster. He was relaxed, and cool, and mellow.

"Like I was saying, thanks to my boy Matthias here, we tracked that account number to another account, here in the good old US. And the best thing about having a bank here in the US is that it requires a name, or a corporation name, which was attached to that account number. But you know, unravel the thread a little bit more, and it turns out the person taking shots at you, the person who embezzled the seventeen point two million from the company, was none other than your CFO."

Royce Blanchard's face went ashen, and he sputtered. "But, b-b-b-ut—"

I shook my head. "It's all here." I flipped the screen in the projector to show how we'd traced the money right back to Royce, and his face went sheet white.

Rafe leaned over to Matthias. "A hundred bucks says he bolts."

Matthias shook his head and whispered back, "That wouldn't end well for him. He knows that. I'll take that bet." They shook hands on it.

Royce looked at the other executives sitting at the table in silence. Then he shoved away from the table, making the chair scrape back as it hit the ground, and he ran for the door.

I just sighed and watched in annoyance as he interrupted my stellar presentation. The other executives in the room were shocked and grabbed their things to keep them from clattering off the desks at the commotion. Royce was headed straight for the exit as if there were anywhere he could really run.

But that was the thing about panicking. A brain in crisis couldn't think, couldn't process. It couldn't walk through all the rational reasons for why it was so dumb to do something. Nope. Instead, fight or flight would kick in. At that point, you would no longer be thinking clearly because your normal synaptic functions would be fuzzy from the shot of adrenaline. It was pure instinct.

Well, it turned out that for Royce, his instincts willed him to run like the wind. And run he did.

Unfortunately for him, he didn't calculate on Tyse, who had been stationed at the door right outside to make sure that nobody went in or out. From my angle, I could see everything. The door opened. Tyse leveled a simple arm bar, and Royce went down like a sack of potatoes.

One blow. Not bad.

I shook my head.

Matthias frowned. "Ugh! Bollocks."

Rafe just chuckled. "Don't worry. I'll give you until we get back to the penthouse to pay up."

I muttered, "Rafe, notice how the kid took him out without having to actually kill him?"

DeMarco rolled his eyes at that. "Oh my God. You try and kill a guy one time, and they never let you forget it."

"Yep. Like Benson here, I'm always going to remember the motherfucker who tried to kill me."

That happened way back when Rafe hadn't always been on our side. He came around eventually, but before that, he had tried to kill every single one of us. Which was a shame really, because I was fucking delightful.

Jonas? Now he maybe deserved to get a bullet every now and then, but me? I was awesome.

Benson stood. "I-I don't understand. So it's over?"

I nodded. "The reports have already been emailed to you, along with your bill."

He blinked rapidly. "I can't believe it. Royce and I started this company together. Why would he do this to me?"

I shrugged. "Oh, you know, greed? There's always someone who thinks they got the bum end of the shaft. Or whatever the expression is."

I could have made some inappropriate jokes right then, but I left it. Besides, it's not for us to determine why someone did something; we just find out who did it and stop it from happening again.

Matthias stood. "Are you sure you weren't supposed to be a performer? You seem to actually like that."

"Yeah, well, you know, sometimes catching the bad guy is fun."

He laughed. "Oh, only sometimes?"

I shrugged. "Sometimes *being* the bad guy is fun."

"Oh, you miss your life of crime?"

I thought about it often. That lifestyle almost got me killed. Even worse? I'd almost lost someone I cared about because I was careless and greedy. When Noah had offered me a way out, I'd taken it and never looked back. Well, almost never. Sometimes I missed the rush of knowing I'd gotten one over on someone. That shit was awesome. But that was the old me. The new me was one of the good guys.

"Nope," I lied. "Not at all."

<hr>

Hailey

I bounced my knee up and down as I mentally ran through my game plan. Next to me, my father clapped his hands. "Hailey. Enough. It's going to be fine."

Yeah, says him. He'd long ago handed off the reins, so it was up to me to please my mother. The launch of the new perfume was just around the corner, and I was drowning. But it had to be perfect, because if it wasn't...

God help us all if it wasn't. I knew what Livingston Perfumes had accomplished over the years. What our name meant in the industry. My nose was mainly responsible for getting us where we were, actually.

"It's fine. Everything's fine."

He chuckled beside me. "You always say that when things aren't fine. Are you sure you didn't get overwhelmed? I promise you, it's going to be great. Your mother loves you no matter what. This does not have to be perfect."

"Yeah, says you, Dad."

I needed to approve the final samples of the latest line. I'd been working on Miriam for over a year. A year of my life with the same scent on my nose.

It was the signature scent that I'd been trying to chase for God only knew how long. Quintessentially my mother. There were hints of bergamot and orange. But it had been the mother of uphill climbs to capture this scent based on the mother I used to know, because Lord knew I didn't recognize her these days.

When the car rolled up to the office, we were driven to the

underground entrance. One of the office security guards, Marlon, opened the door for me. "Good morning, Ms. Livingston. Mr. Livingston."

"Good morning, Marlon."

He beamed, which meant I'd gotten his name right. Thank God. I didn't always pay attention, because I had my nose buried in a book, or was researching something, or was chasing a scent. So sometimes the interpersonal stuff eluded me.

My father stopped in the elevator. Dad and I rode together, but I headed off to the labs on the third floor while he continued to the executive offices. "See you later, sweetheart. Remember, enjoy. Relax. You have accomplished a lot."

I gave him a wan smile even as I waved and walked out. Yeah, perfect. I'd hear about it over and over again.

Relax, it's just perfume.

Yeah, but it wasn't just perfume to me.

She's your mother. She'll love you regardless.

And that was the rub. My mother was difficult at the best of times, and loving me regardless of whether or not I succeeded... well, she wasn't exactly *that* kind of mother. Not anymore. I pushed open the doors to the lab. I was immediately greeted by the fresh, clean scent of nothing.

God, it was so relaxing to walk in and not have the usual scents assailing me. Most everyone at Livingston Perfumes knew better than to actually wear anything scented when they were going to be working with me. But every now and then someone slipped up and wore a bit of perfume. Sometimes it was so overpowering that I wasn't able to work at all.

As Vice President of Product Development, my nose was a huge asset. My father even had it insured. And then of course, well, I hadn't realized how important my nose was until several competitors attempted to poach me in the most bizarre ways possible. I was only twenty-five years old, and already, I'd made a name for myself.

Yeah, but at what cost?

Most of my contemporaries were living a booze-filled, sex-chasing existence. Not me. I had my career established, and I was making amazing strides.

Yeah, but you're lonely, and let's not talk about how your vagina is desolate.

Nope, I was not thinking about my vagina right now. I had work to do. With a smile and a wave to everyone, I walked back to my office, slid off my coat and my shoes, and grabbed my slippers.

Yes, I knew it wasn't professional. But honestly, it was a lab. I didn't need to look fancy down here. Besides, when I went to the antechamber, I needed a fully clean environment and my slippers helped. Of course, everyone followed suit with those little booties on their shoes, so there were no contaminants when I went in to smell.

Once I finished getting ready, I went into the antechamber and smiled at Derrek Jacobson. "Hey Jake, are you ready to do this?"

He grinned. "Yeah, I think this is it. At least I hope so."

"You're a star. Seriously, amazing. How's the baby?"

He grimaced. "Since I was up, I decided to come into work."

"I'm sorry, but at least you'll get some peace and quiet to work here."

He chuckled beside me. "That doesn't make me feel better. I'd give up a kidney for a full night of sleep at this point."

I laughed. The problem was I didn't really understand what he meant. I'd rather work than sleep any day.

But you also have no life. No reason to want to be home.

Something caught my attention, and then I noticed the two people not wearing lab coats in the corner talking to one of my lab technicians.

My brother, Evan. Oh God. What was he doing here?

It's not that I didn't love my brother, but he made it very difficult to like him most of the time.

What the hell was that smell? Too sweet. Pungent. I'd say it was Axe body spray, but I'd pretty much banned it from my brother if he was coming into the office.

God, the overdone citric acid in the solution made my nose burn. Shit. I'd never be able to get that out of my dress. Even the ground coffee beans I'd sniffed wouldn't be enough to clear this out. Shit. I would lose a whole half a day.

"You guys, is someone wearing perfume?"

I was met with silence.

"I'm serious. I get it if someone made a mistake and forgot, but I need to know so I can have you leave and go use the shower upstairs."

Nobody fessed up. Damn it. I needed that person out. If I wanted to get any work done, I couldn't be around them.

My brother rolled his eyes at me. "There goes Princess Hailey, being melodramatic as usual. I swear to God, you make everybody's life so miserable because of that oh-so-special nose of yours."

"Evan, shut up. In case you don't know, I have to do work today. My nose will be ruined for the day if I can't get this person out of here."

He had a very curvy blonde with him. I ignored her.

"Guys, please. Someone admit it."

Again, no one fessed up, so I was forced to walk around the lab, sniffing my employees. Yeah, that's something you don't hear every day.

Table by table, I slowly approached the fifteen that were in there. It was none of them.

Yeah, because they know better.

"Where is that smell coming from?"

My brother came up to me. "Hailey, stop the nonsense. If you just—"

It wasn't him; he knew better. He'd been trained over the years by my father and my mother. Perfume, cologne, and aftershave were only worn in the evening when it couldn't interfere with anybody's work.

I sniffed even closer. He wasn't wearing it, but there was transfer. Maybe the front of his arm? "Evan, did you rub against a perfume stick or something?"

He frowned at me. "Don't be ridiculous."

I ignored him and then took a step closer to the blonde. Oh holy hell, it was her. "Excuse me, are you wearing Glitter?"

She glanced down at her arms. "What? It's kind of early for glitter, don't you think?"

Her voice was soft and feathery, like frosty cotton candy.

"No, not glitter that you see. The perfume called Glitter."

She giggled. "Well, it's my signature. I wear it all the time. I had to buy a lotion. There's even a dry shampoo with it."

I coughed. She came closer, and I practically gagged, trying to get the scent out of my nose.

"Do you recognize that you're in a perfume lab? You're contaminating our ability to work."

She frowned then slid a glance over to my brother. "You were so right. She's a total bitch."

My hand twitched. The temper I kept distinctly and tightly wound and under control attempted to flair to life. *No, don't lose your shit. It's not like he would understand or get it or even care.*

"Well, in that case, allow me to escort you out of my lab."

Evan grimaced because, at the end of the day, he knew I was right. She was interfering with my ability to work, and it was *my lab.* He was my older brother. He should have been the one in charge, but he wasn't. Hell, at this point, he barely even worked for Livingston Perfumes anymore.

"I'm so sorry, Evan. I'm glad you came down to check things out, but I need to ask you to leave so I can work."

Blondie's mouth fell open. She glared at Evan, but he knew I was right, so he couldn't really say anything. "You don't have to be a bitch about it."

I rolled my shoulders. "Time to go, but see you later, okay?" Then I turned my head to the woman at his side. "It was nice not knowing your name."

God, that was so harsh. But really, I needed to get back to work. I had a big day. And I'd already lost hours.

As soon as they marched out—shoulders stiff, chins high—I turned to everyone in the lab. "Sorry about that, guys. Let's go ahead and air out the room. Another two hours and then we'll proceed, okay?"

Everyone nodded. They turned on the air purifiers and started piping in the scent of coffee. Little did they know that wasn't going to help me. I was still too keyed up to even appreciate the gesture. At the moment, the future of Livingston Perfumes was resting on me. And my brother had just robbed me of several precious hours.

CHAPTER TWO

Hailey

By the time I finished the testing for the day, it was after nine o'clock. Not that leaving late was unusual, but I was really feeling it. My feet dragged slightly as I walked across the marble lobby toward the doors. Paul, the night security guard, saw me coming and put his hand to his ear.

"Good evening, Miss Livingston. I already called for your car."

Even though I was exhausted, it was easy to find a smile for Paul. Boyishly charming, he'd been with us for about five years and still wouldn't call me by my first name.

Every time I asked him to call me Hailey, he just grinned and said in his warm southern accent, "I'm from North Carolina. That's just the way we are, ma'am."

"Thank you so much. I'm dead on my feet today."

"Busy around here lately. Everyone's excited about the new perfume. My lady loves the last one."

One of the many benefits we offered to our employees was a huge discount on all Livingston-brand fragrances. Everyone from the part-time mail clerk all the way up to the executive branch should have the opportunity to wear our scents.

There were many advantages to being part of such a prestigious brand. I would never deny the benefits the company had brought to my life: the best education, vacations, and homes that money could buy. But being raised wealthy didn't mean I was blind to the plight of others. It was a simple fact that quite a few of our employees would never be able to afford to wear a Livingston fragrance if we didn't offer such a huge discount. My father had always stressed that this company was like family.

The car pulled up then, so I waved goodbye to Paul and walked out into the humid summer air. The uniformed driver held the door open for me as I climbed into the cool interior of the car. Usually I enjoyed driving myself to work, but whenever I was thick in the testing phase for a new fragrance, my father insisted I use his car service. I balked at first, unwilling to give up any of my hard-won independence, until I almost fell asleep driving home one night.

When I was this tired, it wasn't responsible to be behind the wheel.

The ride passed in a blur, and I could only hope I wasn't rude when I said good night to the driver. My building had a private elevator for the penthouse level, so at least I didn't have to see anyone as I dragged myself upstairs. I waved my keycard in front of the sensor and took a deep breath as the car hurtled upward. It was a struggle to keep my eyes open during the ride. But I had a feeling if I closed them, I might fall asleep standing up. The doors opened with a soft chime.

"Welcome home, Hailey."

The slightly robotic voice came from the built-in speaker directly over my head.

"Good evening, Jarvis."

I'd only had the in-home virtual butler system for a year,

but it still made me chuckle every time I greeted him. The system logged my arrival and turned on lights throughout the penthouse. I dropped my briefcase next to the door and then stepped out of my shoes. Instantly, the pain I'd been ignoring all day flooded through my feet. The pair of limited-edition Louboutins were gorgeous but murder on my toes. Finally, I reached under my blouse and unhooked my bra. It landed on top of my briefcase.

"Feeling better already. Jarvis, remind me to clean up before retiring for the night."

"Noted. Chef left you a plate in the refrigerator. It's your favorite."

The robotic voice followed me, now coming out of a speaker in the kitchen as I went to see what Chef John left for me this time. Cool air bathed my face as I leaned over to peer into the refrigerator. The plate was covered with a thin layer of plastic wrap, but I could easily discern that it was the rosemary lamb chops I loved that practically melted off the bone. I could also tell that the maid service had been by because the Chinese food I had two days ago was gone and the refrigerator was now restocked with milk, eggs and the energy drinks I needed to get through each day.

After a quick detour to my room to change, I returned in my most comfortable pair of yoga pants and a long night-shirt. My dining table was too big and formal for a quick meal, so I set up a place setting on the eat-in counter in the kitchen while the food warmed in the microwave. My thumb rubbed over the tines of the fork, noting how the gold tips were starting to rub off slightly.

"Well, that just won't do." I made a note to have my assistant order new ones just as the room plunged into darkness.

The fork fell from my hand, and the sound of it clattering on the floor was like a gunshot. Disoriented, I placed a hand on the counter in front of me. What had just happened? There hadn't been any mention of storms on the weather report, and it had been clear when I came home.

Then my gaze was drawn to the wide windows on the opposite side of the room where I could see the buildings across the street. All of the windows visible were lit up. If there was a power outage, it wasn't affecting anyone else it seemed.

It was a little odd for a power outage to only affect one building, wasn't it? I stood and walked closer to the windows. From this vantage point I could see more build-ings, and none of them had lost power. Suddenly I felt very vulnerable standing there in the dark.

Then something in the air shifted, and the hair on the back of my neck stood up. I turned slowly, my eyes darting around the room, but it was too dark to see more than a few feet ahead. My head whipped to the side when something moved. What was that? Maybe it was just a shadow, but suddenly I was convinced I wasn't alone.

Panic clawed at my throat, and it was only my hand over my mouth that kept me from crying out.

Think, Hailey!

I had to move because, if someone was in here, I wasn't just going to wait around for them to find me. There was enough light coming in through the windows for me to see the pathway back to the front door.

My phone. I'd dropped my briefcase right next to the door. I crept across the floor slowly, trying not to make a sound. If I could get to my phone, I could call... Honestly, I wasn't even sure who to call. My father? The concierge?

The concierge, of course, made the most sense. There was

probably some sort of building maintenance issue, and I was panicking for nothing.

Then something fell behind me and hit the ground. My heart leaped into my throat. Someone was in here, and they were close.

Too close.

No longer caring about being quiet, I ran, stubbing my toe on something before falling to the ground. Crawling, I almost cried with relief when I felt the unmistakable shape of my bra and then the solid lump of my briefcase. Once my fingers closed over my phone, I turned on the flashlight and waved it around, my heart in my throat.

Nothing. There was no one there.

Hands shaking, I hit the speed dial for the front desk.

"Miss Livingston. Are you calling about the power outage?"

I breathed a sigh of relief. "Yes. So it's not just me?"

"No, ma'am. It's a building wide outage. However, we're recommending that all residents make use of their panic rooms until electricity and property video surveillance is restored."

"Thank you. I'll do that."

After I hung up, I used my phone's flashlight to make my way to the master bedroom. Every one of the units in this building had at least one panic room. Mine had one in the master bedroom and another in the family room. When I bought the place, my father had insisted on it.

At the time I'd protested, telling him that it was unnecessary, but now I was glad to have it. Even if it was a bit ridiculous, it made me feel safer and like I was at least doing something.

Anything was better than standing in the dark and listening to myself breathe. That was enough to freak anyone out.

The panic room in the master bedroom was outfitted with a small couch and several battery-powered lanterns. I brought the pillow and small throw blanket from the end of my bed with me. If I fell asleep waiting for the power to come back, at least I would be comfortable.

As I settled down to wait, I forced myself to take several deep, calming breaths. Why did I always do this? No matter what happened, I always seemed to take it so much more seriously than everyone else. It wasn't like anything had actually happened, after all. The lights had gone out and I'd been forced to make my way in the dark. Big deal. Plus, the building had excellent security. The staff would never allow anyone up who wasn't on my preapproved guest list, so no one except my parents or my brother would ever be allowed up without a courtesy call first.

As my heart rate finally settled, I picked up my phone. I could always work on a crossword puzzle while I waited for the power to come back.

But it was a long time before my heart rate slowed down.

Oskar

"Can we please get the molasses out of our asses? Let's go!"

Rafe ignored me and continued whispering to his wife, Diana. The two of them were always connected at the hip anyway, but it had been even worse since Diana's pregnancy had started to show. She was a badass and an excellent shot. She fought right alongside her husband most of the time, but now that her belly had popped out a bit, it had introduced a whole new dynamic to the team.

Rafe was an overprotective type when it came to her anyway but now... it was like trying to control the direction of a hurricane. Any hint of a threat and he was out of control. Not that I was complaining. Usually all the destructive energy was useful as hell when we were partnered up, but there were times it was inconvenient.

Such as when we were really fucking late for a job.

Times like now.

"For fuck's sake!" I threw up my hands when, instead of ending with a kiss to her forehead, Rafe pulled her closer and started kissing her for real.

The kind of kissing you did when you didn't have to go to work.

"Get a room," Jonas muttered as he walked by then snickered as the two jumped apart.

Diana looked dazed and then mortified when she saw us watching. When Rafe tried to move in again, she planted one hand in the center of his chest. "Uh-uh, big guy. You heard Jonas. Duty calls."

My eyes almost bugged out of my head. "Am I invisible? Is that what's happening?"

Seriously though, what the hell? I had only been standing there for what felt like an hour yelling for Rafe to get the lead out, but all Jonas had to do was say one thing?

My thoughts must have been written all over my face because Jonas clapped me on the back. "Don't take it personally, but he's not going to listen to you when it comes to that kind of thing. He knows I get it."

Jonas's other half was the aptly named Jessica Jones, a ball-busting blonde who, quite frankly, scared us all a little. I could understand if Rafe deferred to him when he needed advice on how to tame a she-devil, but for everything else?

"What does that have to do with anything?"

"It has everything to do with it. Jonas has a lady. He understands." Rafe finally stopped sucking face with his wife and followed us onto the elevator.

We were starting a new job, and this would be our first time establishing the client's routine. Technically she wasn't expecting us for another hour, but I always liked to get us there early so we could scope things out beforehand.

"I may not have a ball and chain, but that doesn't mean I don't understand."

Rafe's obnoxious smirk made me want to cuff him upside

the head. Which I would totally do if he wasn't, you know, an actual former killer.

"Really? Have you ever seen this guy with a woman before?" Rafe turned to Jonas for backup.

"None of my business. Maybe he's got a chick on the side that we've never seen. Or maybe he's into stuffed animals like Matthias. Some things I don't want to know."

Completely unoffended, I laughed right along with them. Our resident tech genius, Matthias, had kept a stuffed animal given to him by his long-lost love that I used to tease him about all the time. Well, no one was teasing him anymore. In a strange twist of fate, that toy had reunited him with his soul mate.

So I guess he got the last laugh on that one.

"Keep guessing about my love life, gentlemen. But I'm not the kiss-and-tell type."

If only they knew how true that was. Over the years, I'd seen and done some pretty off-the-rails shit, but I was never going to be that douche that went around bragging about it. If you were lucky enough to be invited into a woman's bed, you should for damn sure respect her enough to keep it private.

That was just good sexual karma.

We made good time in traffic and pulled into the garage across the street. Noah had negotiated deals with most of the garage companies in the city, so we didn't have trouble finding parking on jobs. I nodded my head as we walked out of the garage and toward the client's address.

"Okay, that's her building. I scoped things out yesterday. One exit in the back through the maintenance room. Fire escape. There's no doorman. Matthias already wired up her security system."

As Rafe ran through the usual details we covered before starting with a new client, my eyes darted left and right, searching for anything or anyone out of place. Being a bodyguard was about so much more than just showing up and intimidating everyone. It was also about the research you put in to understand your client's life and environment. Knowing what was 'normal' in their world made it easier to recognize when something unusual happened.

"Great. This shouldn't take long—"

Just as I reached the door of the building, something whizzed by my right ear and lodged in the doorframe.

"Get down!" Rafe launched himself at me just as another

bullet shattered the glass on the revolving door where I was just standing. We both rolled until we were behind some metal trash cans.

"Fucking hell! Someone's shooting at us already." Jonas's annoyed voice carried over the sound of the panicked screams around us.

People scurried to get out of the way as bullets kept coming, sending a flurry of white dust into the air as they hit the newsstand next to us. The vendor dropped to the ground behind his cart, his panicked eyes meeting mine.

This wasn't good. We hadn't even reached the client yet, and we already had a situation. I pulled out my phone and sent the standard SOS to Matthias so he'd know to send out backup. I glanced over at Rafe. He already had his weapon out, a murderous look on his face.

"We need to get the client back to headquarters. Clearly her ex-husband is even more of a threat than we thought," I added.

He nodded and then motioned to Jonas to cover us. It had been quiet for a few seconds, which could mean the guy was gone or that he was taking time to reload.

"Hurry up, Matthias."

Rafe scowled. "Fuck waiting. We need to make sure this wasn't just a distraction to keep us busy while he's making his way inside."

With just a quick glance over the top of the trash can, Rafe barreled his way toward the revolving door and pushed through. I peered out. Sirens wailed in the distance. We needed to get the hell out of there before NYPD showed up. Noah could deal with them later. Meanwhile, we would already have the client secured.

A few minutes later, a van pulled up to the curb, blocking any further shots. I kept my weapon at the ready, prepared to provide cover once Rafe got the client. After what felt like ages, I saw them coming.

"We got incoming, Jonas."

"Got it."

He automatically took his position on the other side of the van. Rafe came out first, using his body to shield the petite brunette behind him. The van doors opened automatically.

"Go! Go!" Rafe jumped in, and Jonas followed.

With one last glance around, I jumped into the van behind them.

"Never a dull day around here." Matthias smirked as his foot hit the gas, and we screeched away from the curb. He took the first left and then pulled over to the side of the road and put the hazards on.

"What are we waiting on?" I glanced behind us. We hadn't gone far enough to be completely out of the danger zone.

"That." Matthias raised his eyebrows as several police cars raced by heading for the building we'd just left. "They were too close for us to avoid them completely. It made more sense to look like a waiting delivery van than to try to outrun them."

We pulled out into traffic again, and this time Matthias didn't waste any horsepower hauling ass back to the office. Once we pulled in, Rafe jumped out first, extending a hand to the shivering woman in the backseat. Jonas followed.

After they got out, Matthias pulled off and took the van to the back of our garage.

"How the hell did I miss the fact that her husband was this crazy?" Matthias sounded disgruntled.

Everything we did was a team effort, but being the resident hacker meant that Matthias did all the background checks and digging on our clients and the people in their lives. I was shocked that he could have missed something like this also, but I kept that thought to myself.

"People can surprise us. Especially when they're about to be on the hook to pay a ton of alimony."

He shook his head as we walked toward the elevators that would take us up to the penthouse. "I already have Tyse working to find video footage of this shooting. If we're lucky, maybe the asshole walked right in front of a camera before he tried to turn you into Swiss cheese."

"Let's hope."

Our newest recruit had shown interest in the tech side of things, which made Matthias very happy. Hell, it made all of us really happy. None of the rest of us were good at that shit. I was the numbers whiz, and that was enough for me.

When the elevator doors opened, Matthias took off down the hall, probably to go sift through security footage.

Better him than me.

Now that the client was on the premises and secure, I could take a minute to think about the morning's fiasco. We'd been lucky to be there at exactly the right moment, which made me wonder if the soon-to-be ex-husband wasn't the brightest bulb. If he was watching her, shouldn't he realize that the time to attack wasn't when her private security showed up?

The thought bothered me as I continued into the kitchen to find something to eat. Just as I was pulling out sandwich fixings, Matthias appeared.

"Found some footage from another building across the street. It's really weird."

"What?" I looked at the grainy image on his tablet, trying to make sense of what I was looking at.

"That's her building."

Matthias pointed at the shattered window. "Based on the video, the shooter had to be on the roof of one of the neighboring buildings."

It took me a minute to process what he said, but once I got it, I understood why he wanted me to see this. "That's a hard shot. I couldn't even make that shot."

"Exactly. This is crazy. His finances have been under close scrutiny through the divorce proceedings, so how did he manage to hire a sniper?"

As he walked away, still grumbling to himself, I thought about it. Something wasn't adding up, and I hated that. Not only did we have the unanswered question of how this guy had managed to hire a professional, but now there was the more important question of why?

CHAPTER THREE

Hailey

Mentally, I ticked off all the people who I needed to thank. This boutique opening was a soft launch for Never perfume. It was our elegant but accessible line, made for the post-college, first job, professional kind of woman.

I ticked everything off in my head. The displays were perfect, pristine, just as crisp and as fresh as the perfume itself.

My father was in the corner talking to his old friends, the Becketts. James Beckett had started as an investor in

Livingston, but then he'd sold his shares in the company and started sourcing flowers from South Africa.

Across the room, Evan was, well, being Evan. He had the same curvy blonde with him, and both of them had forgone the glasses and were just drinking champagne straight out of the bottle. *Classy.*

I ground my teeth but then forced my jaw to relax. The last thing I needed was an episode of TMJ. Even the slightest ailment to my face threw everything about my sense of smell off. No wonder my father had my nose insured. At first, I thought he was being crazy. It turns out, it was a good idea.

One of the servers brought over a glass of champagne. "Would you like anything else? I noticed you haven't eaten. I can bring you something from the back. There's plenty of food. You know how these things are. No one ever eats." He shrugged.

I gave him a smile and he grinned in return. The dancing light in his eyes told me he was asking about a lot more than if I wanted a canapé. "That's really sweet. But no, thank you. I'm not hungry. This launch has to go well."

He glanced around. I knew what he was thinking. The room was full. The event, for all intents and purposes, was a success. People were clearly drinking and enjoying themselves. The boutique owner, Ella McDonald, had already taken orders from several retail chains in attendance.

But I wouldn't see this as a success until I saw the final numbers. Not until the night was over, the doors were closed, the samples locked away, and I was home behind closed doors. That's when I could call this a success.

"Everyone seems to be enjoying themselves."

"Yeah, of course." He glanced around. "Are you sure I can't bring you something else to eat?"

I shook my head. "I won't be able to eat until this is all over anyway."

"You work at this company?"

I shrugged. "I guess you could say that."

Working for Livingston Perfumes was more than a job. It was a calling. And honestly, where my father was concerned, it wasn't as if I'd had any choice in the matter.

"Oh, what, you're like an intern or something? You know, even interns need to eat, and sometimes interns need to party too."

I blinked at him. "Intern?"

"Yeah, aren't you an intern? You said you sort of work there."

"Oh right." I could have corrected him, but I was too tired, honestly. "Yeah, something like that."

"Well, you know, there's this after-hours spot if you're interested…"

Oh boy. *Yeah, he's asking you on a date. Remember dating?*

No, actually, I couldn't remember dating. Mostly because I hadn't done it much, though it wasn't like I was a virgin.

No dummy. You took care of that in Vegas years ago.

I didn't date much, and when I did, the guys I dated were safe. Kind of boring. No real fire. I'd *almost* married a guy like that. Thankfully, although he'd been initially confused, my fiancé had eventually agreed it was best we didn't get hitched. I'm sure the ironclad prenup my father insisted on also played a part.

You never should have said yes. Steven was dull. Not like him.

I shoved the thought out of my head immediately. I didn't want to think about Steven or the guy who came before him. Yeah, the guys I dated might be boring, but at least none of them had abandoned me in a hotel. So there was that. But I didn't really have time to date. I was too busy.

Excuses. You have pretty much locked away your lady parts and pretended they don't exist.

I rolled my shoulders. I wasn't going to think about that until later. When I was alone. With a good glass of wine. Then I could lament all the choices I'd made to land me at this point. Besides, I wasn't lonely.

My inner diva laughed somewhere deep down in the dark recesses of my soul. *Honey, you've a different idea about what lonely is then.*

I gave my overly friendly server a smile as I went to check on the rest of the guests. Once the event was over, our marketing agent, Mya Taylor, came running over. The Mirage Agency was headquartered in Washington, D.C., but had clients all over the world. Livingston Perfumes was one of their top-tier clients, so we always got preferential treatment, such as their top agents flying out when we needed them.

"Oh my God, Hay! This was such an amazing event."

I wasn't sure how I felt exactly about the nickname, but

Mya was so much fun to be around, always enthusiastic and happy, that I didn't care. She was a little older than I was, but with her curvy figure and long, black braid, she could have passed for way younger.

"Yeah, it worked out really well. Now, on to the big show."

She shook her head in mock dismay. "And I thought I was a workaholic. Can't you just enjoy the fabulousness for one day before you jump right back into the throes of it?"

"Okay, you're right. It went off without a hitch. I'm really happy."

My father was saying goodbye to a few of the last guests. And as far as I knew, Evan had already left with his friend, girlfriend, whatever that girl was. And of course, she'd still shown up at my perfume event wearing Glitter.

God, that perfume was the bane of my existence. It was as ubiquitous as Axe body spray now. It was cheap and accessible and just too much. So sweet, with some cloying citrus added in. Like freaking cotton candy with lemon juice poured on top. It just sat there on the skin. To me, half the time, it smelled like rotting flesh. But far be it from me to criticize anyone else's perfume blend. What worked for one nose didn't always work for another, so I just chose to stay far away from anyone who wore it.

"Sweetheart, you've done fantastic."

I turned to smile at my father. "Thanks, Dad. We were just talking about that."

"And you too, young lady." He shook Mya's hand enthusiastically.

"Thank you, Mr. Livingston. This new perfume is going to become one of my personal favorites. I can't wait to try the new one Hailey is working on."

After a little more chitchat, he checked his watch. "Okay, sweetheart, I'm taking off. I'll send the car back, or are you going to take a taxi?"

"No, you go ahead. I'll call a car. I'm going to just sync up on the last tallies of the night, help them close down, and secure the samples."

He gave me a hug and kissed my forehead. "Well, fantastic job. Text me when you get home so I'll know you're okay."

"Of course, Daddy."

What twenty-four-year-old woman called her father Daddy? Well, he was my father, and it made me feel safe and loved to call him Daddy, so whatever.

The crowds parted, and I could see Milo Hamilton, Mya's

husband, surrounded by a crowd of adoring women. He was one of the few men in attendance so I'm sure he was already regretting joining Mya on this trip. One of the women put her hand on his arm, and I glanced over at Mya uncertainly. Was she seeing this?

Following my gaze, Mya sighed. "That man attracts women like a dog attracts fleas."

I bet that was an understatement. Milo looked like a movie star with dark hair and sky-blue eyes. A man like that was probably used to women throwing their panties at him.

"It doesn't do them any good. The man stares at you like a piece of raw meat. But please apologize on my behalf. He came to keep you company, not to be groped by a bunch of random women."

She snorted. "Don't worry about Milo. The man has no shame. Before we started dating, I actually caught another woman with her hand down his pants. It was a company event, no less. He didn't even bat an eyelash. But that's a story for another day."

I put up one finger. "Um, can that be a story for *today*? Because I have questions. So many questions."

We were both still laughing when Milo walked up. He

looked between us before taking the glass of champagne from Mya's hand. After finishing it in one gulp, he placed it on a nearby table.

"No more of that for you, Mrs. Taylor-Hamilton. You already can't keep your hands off me."

Mya rolled her eyes. "Did you need me to stay, Hailey? We can wait for you."

While she wasn't looking, Milo made exaggerated cutting motions at his neck. I smiled to myself. Clearly, he had plans for his wife that didn't include hanging around this boutique any longer.

"No, the boutique owner is still here. I'm going to check in with her before I call a cab. Thank you again for flying out. Both of you."

After they left, it was just me and Ella Once I had the samples secured in their cases, I thanked her again. "Thank you for offering your boutique for the launch party. I think it was the perfect setting. I can't say enough."

Her cheeks turned slightly pink at the praise. "Oh, really, you did us the favor. Our sales haven't been this high since the holidays. It was a pleasure doing business."

I'd already called for a taxi, so I was expecting it when my phone chimed with a text message alerting me to their arrival.

"All right, my assistant will be in touch. Once the first shipments of our next fragrance come in, you'll get an exclusive for a few days before everyone else."

"Sounds perfect."

"Get home safe."

"You too."

I ran out of the door and glanced around. I didn't see the taxi. When I checked my app, I saw they were around the corner. With a wince and a groan, I skipped down the sidewalk to go and meet them. When I turned the corner, my heart slammed against my chest. At the same time, the hairs on my neck stood at attention, and pure adrenaline flooded through my veins.

My body knew exactly what was happening before my brain even registered it.

An arm wrapped around my waist, and another covered my mouth. I tried to scream, but I couldn't. The sticky stench of sweat and fear burned my nostrils.

I tried to remember every self-defense class my father had

insisted I take, all the anti-kidnap training. But all I could remember was kick, which was really not that useful. I should have kept it up.

I slammed my elbow back into the person's gut. And thankfully, I was pretty heavy, so he *oofed* and loosened his grip just enough for me to be able to bite his finger.

"Son of a bitch."

And with the loosening of the hand in my mouth, I delivered another elbow, and I kept it up until he was forced to let go.

Panting and dizzy, I whirled around and screamed. "Fire! Fire!"

I knew not to scream help. Studies showed that people ignored that. They assumed someone else would call the police and that it was best not to get involved.

But when you said "Fire" everybody responded.

The guy reached for me again, and I threw out a feeble fist. But luckily, the diamond ring on loan from my mother's collection connected with his nose, and blood spurted everywhere. On the silver evening gown I'd worn, all on my face, in my uhhh— in my hair. Blood, so much of it. I flailed some more. The door opened, and I heard a rush of footsteps.

"Hailey? Oh my God, Hailey."

The guy took one look at Ella coming for me, and then he took off down the alley, sprinting. A wave of dizziness and nausea overtook me, and I couldn't stand.

I realized two things. First, I needed to work out more. A little cardio probably would have helped with this whole situation. Second, *oh my God,* I really needed another self-defense class.

You're overreacting.

Even while that voice in my head told me to be rational, and calm, something deeper, something far more primal and instinctual, told me I had not been imagining things the other night when the power went out. Considering that someone had just tried to grab me on the street, I should have listened to my instincts. Instead, I'd rational- ized it away, and now someone had almost hurt me.

But who would have done something like that?

Distantly, I could hear Ella talking to my father. "Yeah, I don't know what happened, but there was this guy, and there's a lot of blood, but I think it's all his. She's fine. She doesn't look hurt, but I don't know... You should probably come back."

I tried to wave my hand and tell her not to do that. But I really was dizzy.

And God, I just wanted to sleep. I wanted to sleep so bad.

I don't know how long it was between the time Ella made the call and when I heard my father's voice in my ear. All I knew was that I sat with my back against the brick wall.

"Sweetheart? Baby, are you okay?"

"Dad?"

"Do you see what I mean? I absolutely need to hire a security team. It's not safe for you to be out on your own."

"Dad, it's okay. I just—I have to be more careful."

"Enough. In the morning I'm calling the top security firm in the city. You really want to tell me you can handle this yourself?"

I knew he was right. I didn't want to it to be true, but I knew. I hadn't just been paranoid the other night. Someone *had* been in my home. "Yeah." I nodded. "Make the call."

Even as I said the words, I knew I could pretty much kiss my freedom goodbye.

Oskar

I hadn't slept much. I kept running through the events of the previous day over and over in my head. Something was... off. What had we missed?

I knew I was obsessing, but it was like finding a number out of place. Counting wasn't exactly sexy, although I clearly made it look good. But it was about solving the puzzle, making something fit. Sure, I liked to do things with a little flair, but I still needed the numbers to make sense to me. And something about last night certainly didn't make sense.

A set of fingers snapped in front of my face. "Oskar, what the fuck is wrong with you?"

I turned my glare on Noah, giving him my fiercest scary-Viking face The problem was Noah, having been a former killer himself, he wasn't afraid of anything. Well, except his wife. And his daughter. Actually, come to think of it, we were *all* terrified of Izzy when she cried.

Considering we were an entire office full of bad asses, the fastest way to bring any of us to our knees was a screaming Izzy.

"Is there something you need?"

"Yeah. We have clients coming."

From the kitchen island, I glanced over at the conference room. Yup, it was certainly set up for a client meeting. "Who's the client?"

"You haven't been paying attention to anything I've said, have you?"

I shook my head. "Sorry, I was just thinking about yesterday. I can't make the numbers add up, so it's bugging me, I guess. Who's coming in?"

"Corporate security gig. Real high rollers. I'm talking billionaire status."

"Oh, okay. Do you need me on this job?"

Noah stared at me like I'd lost my mind. "Are you okay? Do you need some days off or something? What the fuck is wrong with you?"

Asshole. "What's wrong with me is I'm the best fucking

motherfucker in this house. I'd actually like some kind of commendation if you don't mind."

Noah just rolled his eyes. "Yes. I need you on this job. But if you've got something going on, then tell me. I'll rearrange the others. Give Tyse more of an active role."

I shook my head. "Nope, he's untested. Besides, I'm fine. I'm just trying to wrap my head around something yesterday. The fucking puzzle is killing me, but I'll figure it out. Yeah, I'll be there for the meeting."

Noah just shook his head. "Have you forgotten how this works? I meet the client, then bring in the team. Seriously, are you okay?"

He had a point. My mind was completely off. I'd slept like shit. Tossed and turned all night. I just didn't feel like myself.

"Yeah, fine. Go on, I'll be right there, or come get me when you need me, rather." I corrected myself.

Noah sauntered off. He slid me a glance again. No doubt he was going to go ask the kid if I'd lost my shit. Well, I didn't like being shot at. I was too pretty to die young. And to be honest, people had shot at me plenty since I'd taken this job. Angry ex-boyfriends, angry husbands, angry wives, royalty, all manner of people. Replaying what happened yesterday, it felt like I'd missed something, like there was a big gaping clue that I'd tripped over and missed it, and now my brain couldn't connect the two dots.

I wondered if I should brew another cup of coffee, like I needed any more. I was so jittery. While I waited, I grabbed a mug from the cabinet and then stopped.

What was that smell?

Something light. Distinctive. Crisp. Ultra-feminine. What was that? The scent immediately took me back to years ago when my life was different, when I'd been a different person.

When you fell for a girl and nearly got the both of you killed.

The scent was so distinctive. Just a whiff of it and immediately, my blood rushed to my dick, making my cock thick and heavy. The last thing I needed before a fucking meeting.

Get your shit together.

The coffee timer pinged, and I went to get my cup, not realizing I already had a mug in my hand.

If I didn't get my shit together, Noah was going to think we had a problem. And considering where I'd come from, I never wanted to give him any reason to think so. We might not always see eye to eye on the best methodology for things, but I had a home here.

And truthfully, I wasn't the head case in the group. It was never going to be my turn to lose my shit.

So, get it together. Stop thinking about that long-ago weekend. It's over. You're never going to see her again.

CHAPTER FOUR

Hailey

I glanced over at my father, gauging whether I should bother reasoning with him. Not that it worked at all the last few times I'd tried. He was set on the idea that I needed security, and after what had happened at the event, he wouldn't be swayed.

He's worried. Be understanding, Hailey.

I sighed. I was really trying. My father had always been very protective. It was sweet if a little suffocating. But things had been different when I was a child and naïve to the ways of the world. He'd been right to be concerned that I might not be wary enough of people's motives.

There were plenty of people who'd tried to get close to me only to meet my father or to try to get access to corporate secrets. There had been a time when I needed protection from the opportunists of the world.

But not anymore.

I wasn't the type to trust easily. Life had proven over and over that most people were just out to get what they could. I'd learned to take care of myself.

Suddenly cold, I hugged my arms closer, trying to ward off the memories of the man who'd driven that lesson home so thoroughly. Oskar had been a mistake, but I couldn't bring myself to really regret it. He'd broken my heart, but he'd also taught me not to let my guard down. Our time together was the quickest life lesson I'd ever learned but one I would never forget. Hot men with muscles coming out of their ears might be perfect for a weekend of fun as long as you didn't make the mistake of thinking it was more than that.

In the years since that fateful weekend, I'd buried myself in work and learned more about myself and what I wanted. I'd also avoided men pretty well.

Now I would have to deal with some overgrown jock following me and trying to order me around. No thanks.

"This is it. Mr. Blake is expecting us." My father's voice cut into my thoughts.

I looked up to see that while I'd been brooding, our car had pulled into an underground garage. I climbed out, running a nervous hand over my hair. I didn't sleep well last night, and it felt like every one of those fretful hours was showing on my face. But I couldn't let my father see that. He was already losing it and he didn't need any more evidence that I couldn't take care of myself.

"Don't you think this is a bit much, Dad? I thought we'd just have one of the security guards in the building walk me to my car each night. I didn't think you were serious about hiring an outside firm."

He pulled out his phone. "He sent me instructions. Oh yes."

I followed him, almost tripping over a chip in the asphalt as I struggled to keep up with his fast pace. "What is the hurry? I thought you said we were early?"

Dad stopped at the elevator bank and then entered a code on the keypad on the wall. The elevator doors opened. He smiled.

"I can see they really do take security seriously. Very promising."

It took all my effort not to roll my eyes. Not that I didn't think my father was serious about my safety, but I was pretty sure he was also enjoying the cloak-and-dagger business a bit too much. All the James Bond security measures seemed a bit overdone in my opinion. Why did we need a code just to access the elevator? Was Blake Security expecting a team of assassins to try to break in at any moment?

The thought was so absurd it made me smile.

My smile dropped away when the elevator doors opened and we were greeted by an intense-looking man with dark hair and eyes.

Holy moly.

I took a step back instinctively before I caught myself. If this was Noah Blake, then I could see why his security company was so successful. Not too many people would get on his bad side.

"Mr. Livingston. Miss Livingston. I'm Rafe DeMarco. Welcome."

My father accepted the handshake Rafe offered. "Thank you. I'm very happy you were able to accommodate us."

Rafe glanced at me so quickly I almost missed it. "Of course. Considering the circumstances, we understand the urgency."

Something passed between him and my father that let me know they'd been talking about me. Great.

After showing us to a modern waiting area, Rafe disappeared around a corner, leaving me free to gawk openly. The building looked industrial from the outside, and I could see the evidence of that inside, too. Exposed pipes and beams gave the space a rustic vibe but the glass walls and gleaming chrome detailing also made it look futuristic and hi-tech at the same time. It was an interesting combination.

The man who approached was just as intense as the last guy but at least made the attempt to smile.

"Noah Blake. And this is my colleague Jonas Castillo. He'll be joining us as we assess your security needs."

After shaking our hands, the men gestured for us to follow. It was while we were walking down the hallway, my father happily chatting to Mr. Blake, that my famed stubbornness finally kicked in. I'm not sure what took her so long to show up, maybe it was just fatigue, but somewhere between the handshakes and the conference room door, I stopped walking.

"No. No way. This has gone far enough. I don't need a bodyguard."

Dad turned around, his forehead already creased in the way it did when he was worried. "Now, Hailey..."

But it was Noah who answered my father. "Mr. Livingston, we are very interested in your daughter's perspective on this. As the target, she will be integral to helping us understand her security needs. If she doesn't feel that she's at risk, we need to know why."

Shocked that he was defending me, even if it might mean losing business, I felt some of my anger drain away.

"I just think this is overkill, that's all. I almost got mugged. Of course it was scary, but this is New York. These things can happen. It's just part of life in the city."

My passionate response was interrupted by a long, loud yawn. Embarrassed, I clapped a hand over my mouth to try to cover the sound.

"Sorry. I haven't been sleeping so well."

"Understandable. Jonas, why don't you show Miss Livingston to the break room for a coffee."

The nice one took my elbow gently and steered me back the way we came. I glanced over my shoulder to see my father and Mr. Blake disappear into the conference room.

"Smooth. Your boss might as well have patted me on the head and told you to occupy the little lady while the men talk."

That seemed to give Jonas a lot of enjoyment. "Trust me, if you'd ever met his wife, you wouldn't think so. She'd kick his ass for just the thought."

I snorted a little at that. But I had to admit, knowing that Mr. Blake was married changed my opinion of him a little. Although I couldn't imagine how tough his wife must be if she could handle him.

Jonas handed me a cup of coffee.

"Thank you." I busied myself adding a lump of sugar and a small packet of creamer.

"While Noah assures your distraught father that his only daughter isn't in imminent danger, why don't you tell me why you're so opposed to having security as a precaution."

My shoulders slumped. "Do they train you guys to guilt people into hiring you?"

He grinned. "That depends on whether or not it's working."

Jonas leaned on the counter next to me. "You might think I'm guilting you, but you weren't here when your father's call came in. He's worried about you. Would it really be so bad to have someone around to watch your back?" He nudged my arm gently.

I couldn't resist smiling back. Jonas had the kind of uncomplicated beauty and sophistication that could put anyone at ease. It wasn't hard to see why Noah had tasked him with calming me down.

Suddenly Jonas stood up straight. "Oh, the rest of the team is here. I'll be right back."

I turned to see who he was talking about and almost dropped the ceramic mug in my hand. But instead my fingers tightened around the handle, and I shoved years of hurt, humiliation and rage down beneath the ice-princess façade that had always served me so well.

And prepared myself to face the only man I'd ever loved.

Oskar

I had to be going crazy.

I shook my head, rolling my shoulders to release the tension that had gathered there in the last few minutes. After arriving home from a difficult job, all I usually wanted to do was relax. But there was something stopping me. Something in the air that made me think about nights gone by and lost moments.

The last time I'd smelled something that stopped me in my tracks, I'd been much younger and more optimistic.

Stupider, too.

I was ashamed at the thought, but there was also a part of me that missed the days when I'd believed that anything was possible. Every time I thought of Hailey, I tried to remember the good things such as how she made me laugh and how for the first time, I believed that I could outrun my past.

That was, of course, before it all went to hell.

Wanting to believe the best had almost gotten an innocent

woman killed. It was something I'd never forgotten again. Guys like me didn't get to ride off into the sunset. We're perpetually part of the night.

That's what being in the underworld does to you.

Usually I was pretty good about keeping the past in the past. But all it took was a whiff of a perfume that reminded me of Hailey, and I'd gone straight back there. Maybe I was just hungry. I turned the corner into the kitchen and then stopped. Jonas was leaning close to a young woman, talking in a low, soothing voice.

He was good at this part, calming down distraught people, helping them to sort through the things going on in their lives so they could make decisions. It had to be partially because of his former career as a police officer, but some of it was just his personality. He was pretty calm in general, unlike Noah, who was bottled fire, and Rafe... Well, that dude was just a volcano waiting to erupt.

Me, I was more like a mountain. I could joke around with the best of them, but I kept my feelings to myself. I wasn't the best one to calm a scared woman down because more than likely I'd say the wrong thing or make an inappropriate joke that would get me pulled into a meeting with Noah.

Hey, that only happened once or twice. Okay, maybe four times.

But in this case, I wasn't interested in Jonas working his magic. All of my attention was on the woman. The long fall of her curly, dark hair, the cinnamon hue of her skin, and the smile that I already knew was potent enough to stop any man in his tracks.

But it was the eyes that were the killer. The eyes, which were right now trained on the mug in her hands, were as dark as coffee beans and so big I'd seen every dream I'd ever had in them. Those eyes had once looked at me like I was her savior and her every naughty fantasy rolled into one.

It was going to hurt like hell when I saw them now because I was no longer her dream. I was the guy who'd abandoned her.

Jonas saw me first, saying something to her that made her nod absently. Then she looked up, and for just a second, I saw a flash of what we'd once shared. Hope. Excitement. And pure joy.

How long had it been since anyone had looked at me like that?

"Oskar, we have a new client. The Livingstons. They're a big-time jeweler on Fifth Avenue." Jonas was talking but I barely heard a word.

I was still locked in an epic battle of eye warfare with Hailey. *If looks could kill* was an apt phrase for the way she was glaring at me.

Then, just as suddenly, all the animosity on her face disappeared. She blinked once and then smiled. "Oskar. How are you?"

Jonas looked between us, confused. "You know each other?"

"Yes."

"Barely."

We answered at the same time, Hailey's annoyance making a brief appearance before she locked it down again underneath a placid smile.

"We knew each other years ago," I finally responded.

Jonas made a soft sound. "Okay then. I'm going to check in with Noah and Mr. Livingston. Hailey, I'll be right back."

Her frozen smile stayed in place until Jonas turned the corner down the hallway. Then she turned away slightly, focusing all of her attention on the mug in her hands as if it was the most fascinating thing in the world.

"So..." She seemed to flounder before regaining her confidence. "How, uh... how are you?"

"Are you really going to pretend we're nothing more than acquaintances? I think we're past the *how are you* stage."

Even though I understood exactly why she was freezing me out, I wasn't prepared for the way it would make me feel. It seemed so wrong that she was treating me like some stranger or an old classmate. Not like I'd once had her panties between my teeth.

Hailey sniffed. "I know you. That's why I asked how you were. But no, I don't think we're past the *how are you* stage. Waking up alone showed me we don't know each other at all."

With just one sentence, she unwittingly revealed just how much I hurt her that day. And even though I couldn't, the urge to explain was so strong it felt like I was vibrating from holding myself back. But what could I really say?

I'm not a good guy.

You deserved better.

Being with me put you in danger.

I left to protect you.

The first two things she undoubtedly already knew, and the last two things would lead to questions I couldn't answer. There was only one path forward for us, and it was down the road of no return. It was good that Hailey hated me because it would make it easier for us to keep our distance. That was the best thing I could do for her, despite the fact that her glare made me feel like my soul was rotting from the inside out.

"You're right."

She looked shocked, but before she could say anything else, we heard voices. Noah, Jonas, and a man I assumed was Mr. Livingston came around the corner. Noah paused when he saw how close Hailey and I were standing. I took a step back and worked to get myself under control.

"Mr. Livingston, this is Oskar Mueller." Jonas made the introduction since Noah was still staring at me.

"Nice to meet you, sir." I shook Mr. Livingston's hand, trying to think of a subtle way to get out of this without making Noah suspicious. I'd just finished another job, so there was no logical reason that I couldn't be on Hailey's case.

Other than the fact that I still had a hard-on for her that wouldn't quit, and I fully expected her to knee me in the balls at any moment.

"He's going to be your primary contact, provided that Miss Livingston agrees." Jonas gave Hailey a look that I didn't understand.

But it must have meant something because she sighed and then nodded.

"Okay, I guess it wouldn't hurt to have someone watching my back."

Noah looked satisfied. "We're very discreet. Our goal is to help you maintain your lifestyle and typical routine with as few interruptions as possible. Ideally, you won't even notice we're there."

"Let's just get this over with." She picked up her mug and walked back into the kitchen.

Mr. Livingston looked apologetic. "Sorry. My daughter doesn't think all of this security is necessary."

I wondered how long it would take for the man to realize

that his daughter's reluctance was about more than just having security in general. But I couldn't ask too many questions. Airing our dirty laundry wasn't going to help anyone and would only draw attention away from the reason they were there.

And just like that, everything inside me went ice cold. My shock at seeing Hailey again had blinded me to the most obvious question. Why was she here?

What had happened that would cause her to need security?

CHAPTER FIVE

Hailey

I knew what was happening. It was a panic attack. The booming heartbeat in my skull, the short rapid breath, the headache looming just behind my eyes, and the faint dizziness. I was having a panic attack over a man.

Not just any man. That man. What the hell was he doing here? Why was he here? After all these years, why did he have to just reappear without any warning?

If only I'd known and been better prepared, I could have, *I don't know*, girded my loins. But there he was, looking just as gorgeous as before. He looked older now. No, older wasn't quite it. Kind of like he'd filled out a little bit more to become... Well, he'd become a man.

Oh, he was a man then.

All kinds of a man. Hell, he'd been the only marker I really had for what a man was. But there was something about him now, something even more self-assured. That insanely strong jaw. Those pure blue eyes, ice blue, I'd always called them. That pale blond hair marking him every bit the Viking. With his enormous height, the idiot looked like Thor.

How was I supposed to resist Thor? It was like my inner diva finally woke up, and she was starting to have feelings.

No time for feelings. Shut it down. That man left you alone in a hotel room after what you thought was the hottest weekend of your life.

Which it technically was because I'd never had another experience like it.

God, I needed to get it together. Deep breaths, in and out. Everything would be fine. My father would handle things with Blake Security. After I walked out, obviously he'd see that we weren't suited, he would find me someone else, and I would never have to see Oskar Mueller again.

What are the odds?

By the time my father made it back down to the car, I was calmer. My heart rate had returned to normal. I was less panicky, less dizzy too. I knew what a little distance from Oskar Mueller could do for a girl.

I expected my father to ask me a whole slew of questions on the way back to the office but... nothing. Instead, he chatted amicably about the Miriam perfume and kept me talking about last night's opening. I could tell he was dancing around the topic. He wanted Miriam to be mine alone.

And it was. It was my baby. It was the first perfume I had conceptualized, done the research on, and picked the scents for completely by myself. I'd also done all the marketing for it. It was mine, with zero input from anyone else.

I was proud of it. I was also completely terrified. I needed everything to be perfect. Having a random violent stalker was not conducive to that.

Stop jumping to conclusions. You don't have a random violent stalker.

Oh yeah? What do you call the guy who tried to grab you on the street?

Okay, admittedly, security might be a good idea. It was a rational choice and option. I really couldn't argue that. But I didn't want anyone who was going to interfere in my life. I wanted someone who was going to blend into the background. Obviously, since Blake Security hadn't worked out, we'd have to find someone else.

Which was fine.

Are you sure it's fine? Or do you want to go back and ask Oskar where the fuck he went?

There had been an irrational, childish part of me that had wanted to smack that insanely chiseled jaw and scream about where the hell he'd gone, how he could have left me. There was that childish part of me that wanted to hurt him as much as he'd hurt me. I wanted him to pay for all the lonely nights I'd spent wondering what I did wrong.

That part of me had all types of vengeance planned for Oskar Mueller.

But rational me prevailed. I was never going to see him again. So there was that. And what the hell was he doing in New York anyway? Wasn't he from Vegas or something?

Be honest, you didn't know much about each other.

That was true, so I'd marked him as a moment of temporary insanity and moved on. I could bury this. I'd survived for years without thinking about him.

When we returned to the office, Dad walked me to mine. He wanted to get a gander at Miriam. I'd been keeping him away up until now, but having his opinion certainly wouldn't hurt.

When we reached my office, I stopped abruptly. The door was open.

I paused. Had someone broken in?

But I didn't need to worry about that. No one had broken in. It was just my brother, Evan, sitting at my desk.

When he saw me and Dad, he threw his hands up. "Seriously? Dad, we had a meeting."

My father frowned. "Evan, didn't you get my messages? I left them with your assistant. There was an incident at the boutique last night, so I took Hailey to meet a security company."

Evan's gaze shifted. "What do you mean, *incident*?"

Evan had all the markers of concern: furrowed brow, lips pressed into a firm line, hands on his hips, in the defensive, territorial position. He was pissed. But was it that someone had tried to hurt me or that I was with Dad? I hated that it was even a question, but hey, truth was truth.

"Yeah, I don't know what it was about. Maybe it was about Miriam. Or maybe something else, but they didn't get anything."

"Are you fucking serious?"

I sighed and then slid behind my desk, moving him aside gently. When he wasn't looking, I quickly adjusted the pens that he always unsorted so that they were back in color-coded order. I straightened my notebook, moved the tissue box where it belonged, and cringed at the colorful paper clips that were now disorganized.

I'd have to fix that one later.

"And yes, I was serious. Someone tried to grab me outside the boutique."

His eyes went wide. "You're fucking serious."

"I swear to God, Evan, who would make a joke about this?"

My father was much calmer, as he always was. "Evan, I'm sorry I missed our meeting. We can meet now."

Evan threw his hands up. "Dad, I'm not that much of a prick that when something happened to Hailey, I don't care."

Dad and I exchanged a quick glance. We were both thinking the same thing. *Aren't you though?*

Evan apparently caught Dad's expression and shook his head. "Fine, whatever. You know what? I don't want to meet with you anyway. I had a great idea, but clearly, you don't want to hear it." And then he stormed out.

Dad called out after him, "Evan, come back." But my brother was in no mood.

"Dad, you should go after him."

My father frowned as if he wasn't sure what the right solution was.

"Dad, he's upset. We can talk about Miriam later."

"Are you sure, baby?"

"Yes. Go fix Evan."

I had to watch my father go after my brother. I sighed at the inevitable familiarity of it all. This, too, was something I knew well. Evan never felt like he was being seen, and then my parents would have to chase after him. And well, there wasn't much that I could do about it. He was my brother, and I actually didn't want him upset, because I did love him.

Yeah, but where does that leave you?

It left me where it always did. All alone, with no idea how things had gone so wrong.

Oskar

This was not part of the plan.

I had been very clear with Noah that assigning me to her was going to be a bad idea, especially after the way we left things and the way she pretended that she barely knew me in the office.

Luckily, Rafe or Matthias—hell, *anybody* else—hadn't seen that. Otherwise, I would never hear the end of it.

Never. When it came to doling out shit, I preferred to be on the giving end of things. Though it was probably only a matter of time before Jonas let that little bombshell drop.

I ran my hands through my hair. Whether she wanted security or not, she needed it. Noah said there had been a threat to her life. Someone had grabbed her. Just that knowledge made me want to get some wet work training from Matthias.

News flash, dumbass: you don't know her.

Wasn't that the truth? I'd left her to protect her from the shit in my past that was headed her away. And clearly, she was pissed off about it, which she should be. What I'd done was shitty. And it was even shittier that I *had* to do it.

The guy she met in Vegas was all carefree and fun. Yeah, that was me. But there had been this whole other side I hadn't told her anything about.

News flash, dumbass: you don't generally have flings when your father is the forensic accountant for dangerous criminals the world over, and you're his protégée possibly even better than the old man himself. Every now and again, those criminal elements got a wee bit ticked off because they thought they should have more money than they really did. After all, it wasn't my fault they spent all their money on hookers and cocaine.

But no, I thought I had been protecting her. And I had been. But now she was back in my life like a tsunami, and I had no idea what to do.

I heard the familiar clip clop of her direct stride. A smile tugged at my lips as I remembered that long-ago Vegas night when I'd seen her. There was no coyness about her, no fluff. Just this extreme femininity paired with cold efficiency. I loved the dichotomy, and I couldn't help but stare at her. There was something so soft and utterly feminine about her, about the way she approached things. All brain, all rational thinking. And here she was again. The woman I'd thought was just a marker. A blip in my life.

She was back, and it burned to see her again. It bore a hole in the center of my chest that I knew I wouldn't be able to wish away. She was searing her way through my inner organs and I didn't have a chance.

She was none too pleased to see me. "What the hell are you doing at my office?"

"Well, you see, butterfly, this is how it works. Some idiot with a grudge to bear against your father or your company, tries to hurt you. Me, *big bad security Viking guy,* makes them go away in a very painful manner so they won't be able to repeat the experience. That's how it works."

She lifted a brow. "I didn't approve this."

I grinned. "That's the joy of this whole thing. You see, you don't need to approve it. I've been paid, so I'm not going away." Also, there's no way I was letting her go away when I knew someone was trying to hurt her.

So much for not wanting the assignment.

"I assumed that my father would see that Blake Security wasn't a good fit."

I shrugged. "Guess not. I'm here. So how we're going to do this is, I've already taken a good look at your office arrangement here. I'm going to follow you home, check out your loft, and see what security measures and adjustments we need to make."

She lifted a brow. "The hell you are. I wasn't warned about this. I need time."

"I'm sorry. You don't have time. You think you had time last night when that guy tried to grab you off the fucking street?"

Anger seeped into my tone. I didn't mean for it to, but I

was pissed off that someone had his hands all over her. And she had the nerve to be arguing about who was watching her ass right now.

She swallowed hard, and as she marched to the door, I heard her mutter, "I don't need some huge Viking asshole following me everywhere."

I grinned. Yeah, still Hailey. She didn't swear much, but when she did, it was all under her breath. Not like she was apologizing for it, but because she knew she wasn't supposed to. But she still had to give voice to her feelings, so she always muttered it right under her breath. And half the time, if you weren't listening, you would miss it.

Stop it. This is not the Hailey memory lane, yellow brick road shit. You don't get to revisit this. Do your job.

I cleared my throat. When we got to the parking garage, Tyse stepped out of his car. He was double parked close to Hailey's VIP parking spot.

"Hailey, this is Tyse. He's going to follow us to your place and handle a perimeter search of your apartment building."

She slid a glance to Tyse and had a smile for him. "Nice to meet you. But honestly, this seems excessive. Already, I don't like it. And we weren't supposed to hire Blake Security anyway. I had no idea this was going to happen today."

"Yeah well, it's happening."

I could tell she wanted to say something, but instead, she walked to her car and plopped into the front seat with all the petulance of a three-year-old. Then she angrily punched the ignition key in the car. The sleek Mercedes hummed to life, and she slammed the door.

Tyse lifted his brows and chuckled under his breath. "Oh, I see you made an impression. It's weird, because women usually love you."

I shrugged. "This one does too. She just doesn't remember."

Tyse's brow furrowed, but I wasn't in the mood to answer. Instead, I slid into the passenger's seat of her car. The last thing I needed was to remember everything about her, because I had a job to do here.

And the hardest part of it was going to be keeping my fucking hands off of Hailey Livingston.

CHAPTER SIX

Hailey

First observation: Oskar Mueller was still melt-your-panties gorgeous. Second observation: He was still annoying. He had this way of crawling under your skin and worming his way in.

I still remembered the night I met him. He'd been annoyingly persistent. Not pushy. Just subtly charming. I'd first been stunned by his good looks and wondered if he was, in fact, talking to me. But then I'd sort of felt *compelled* to talk to him. He was just enough of a tease to make me curious. And before I knew it, there he was under my skin and I was following him all over Las Vegas, acting like a crazy person.

And also, boning. *Much* boning.

My tummy squeezed. God, when was the last time I'd boned someone? Hell, kissed someone, felt special? Had someone's full attention like that?

You really don't want the answer to that.

As gorgeous as he was, I was annoyed that he was poking through my things. I knew what he was doing. He was trying to see if I was the same. He kept touching things, like candles and little silver frames. Adjusting things just a smidge.

It's fine. I do not need to fix it. It's totally fine. I will fix it in the morning. Even better, I will show him that what he's doing is not working. Because I don't need to—

Oh, fuck it, I did. I stood, following behind him and adjusting everything so it was back in the right place.

At the other bookcase, he stopped and turned to face me, the laugh making the corners of his lips twitch. "Your place is still perfect, butterfly."

I huffed, ignoring him. I hated that nickname.

You love *that nickname.*

"Do you want a drink?" I stalked away to the kitchen. Maybe if I could make myself a drink, I would feel better.

"Nope. I'm on duty."

I whipped around, and he was right freaking behind me.

"You move entirely too quietly for someone so big."

He grinned like an idiot. "You've said that before."

"You know what? Can we just stop this whole walk-down--memory lane thing? I don't want to."

"You know what? It's not like this is a walk in the park for me either. I'm doing my job."

"Then do your job. Stop trying to... I don't know, get to me."

He lifted a brow and grinned. And swear to God, one of my ovaries exploded.

"So, I'm getting to you?"

His smirk was all swagger and charm and pure *drop your panties, set them on fire, and spread your legs* kind of sexy.

"You're impossible." I whipped back around and then tripped over his freaking shoes, right on the edge of my living room.

It all happened so quickly. I put my arms out to attempt a forward fall-break, which I'd never been very good at in self-defense class.

But as it turned out, I didn't need to remember my self-defense classes after all. His strong arm wrapped around me, pulling me back against him. Before I knew what was happening, I was in the strong bands of Oskar's arms, and my body was pressed against his, and... Jesus Christ, I didn't know what it was, but his scent didn't bother me. He was wearing a cologne, but it was so subtle. It mixed with his natural scent, smelling like ocean breezes and something smoky and delicious that made me want to take a bite and—

"Stop it."

He stared down at me. "What do you mean?"

"You're looking at me like I'm dessert."

His gaze skipped down to my lips again. "That's because I've been a good boy eating all my vegetables. And I fucking missed you."

His lips slanted over mine, and the shot of pure lust into my system weakened my knees. That was the only explanation for it, because when his tongue slid over mine, God help me, I moaned. I was being a complete moron. I didn't know him. And he was kissing me expertly, I might add.

I whimpered as my body melted into his. God, I just wanted to —

NO! No, you don't. Remember? He left you all alone in a hotel room.

That was just the splash of cold water I needed. I wrenched my lips from his and shoved my hands against his chest.

"No. We are not doing this. My father has backed me into a corner about accepting security, and I can see that I need it. He's worried. Fine. But I don't trust you. I going to ask for someone else, so don't you go getting comfortable." I shoved harder against his chest, but he didn't move.

Only then did it occur to me that I was really going to need for him to listen to me, because there was no way I was getting out of Oskar's arms unless he was letting me.

Finally, he slowly eased back, his jaw tight. "As you wish, butterfly."

There was so much sadness and want in his eyes, but I was not falling for it, because I had fallen for it once before.

I bent and picked up his shoe. "This is why I like things in their place. I almost broke my neck falling over these big boats."

He grinned at me. "Well, you know what they say about men with big feet."

I was so tempted to throw it at him the shoe twitched in my hand.

I forced myself to take a deep breath and then I forced another one. I took the fury that coursed through my blood it and dismantled it. I asked myself the question, *what will you get if you throw the shoe at his head, besides satisfaction?* When I came up empty, I bent down and picked up the other shoe and then walked them over to the sideboard.

I opened one of the drawers that opened at an angle. "This is where the shoes go. This is the guest drawer."

His bark of laughter was fresh. "Wait, you have a special drawer marked for guests so they can put their shoes away?"

"Yes, it's perfectly rational. No one wants shoes everywhere. This is New York. Closet space is at a minimum."

He grinned at me. "God, some things never change."

I leveled a direct glare at him. "But some things are irrevo-cably broken, and you can't go back."

Then I marched down the hall to my bedroom and quietly closed the door.

Oskar

In hindsight, maybe kissing her wasn't the best idea I'd ever had because now there would be no getting her taste off my tongue.

I remembered just how long it had taken... not to forget her, but to shove her back to the far corners of my mind where I didn't think about her every minute, then every hour, then every day. Finally, it became weekly, then monthly. Eventually, the fleeting thoughts about her, complete with pangs of regret, didn't filter into my consciousness regularly, just every once in a while, with a slice of heat so intense it made me want to do something to forget.

But now I'd be starting from ground zero again. *Yeah, way to go.*

When she went to shower, I finished checking the rest of the condo. When I'd met her, her hotel room had been nice, but then, so was mine. I hadn't really stopped to think and ask what exactly she did that she could have a penthouse suite. But now, as I pieced together the little parts of her past I hadn't known at the time, it all made sense.

Her loft was just as nice as that Las Vegas penthouse, complete with stellar views of Central Park. Crisp, contemporary design aside, her place was pristine. Everything had its place. Contemporary furnishings, nothing too frilly, but still exquisite.

I might look like a Viking, but I appreciated the finer things in life. After all, I'd been taught to appreciate them.

You've also been taught to steal them.

Nope, not me anymore. And just because I had seen Hailey again didn't mean I needed to revert to my old self. *New rule: no more touching her. Ever.* Besides, touching her would mean I wanted to do more. I was hardly the permanent guy, which was something that Hailey needed.

What if you could be the permanent guy?

Even if I could, she would never trust me. So, there was that.

The door to her bedroom opened, and Hailey came out in soft looking pajamas. There should have been nothing sexy about the boxy cut, but still, it made me flash back to that weekend. Every time she'd tried to put on clothes, I'd taken them from her and hid them. So she'd been forced to walk around naked, hair wild, with bite marks all over her gorgeous, brown skin. I swallowed hard and shoved that thought aside.

"Do you need anything?" she asked.

"No, I'm good."

"I didn't expect you. The guest room is currently full of samples. I don't even have a bed in there. No one stays here. I'll get someone to bring a bed later for whoever ends up staying. You'll have to take the couch for now."

As she averted her gaze, I had to smile at that. "Oh, I'll take the couch for now, unless you invite me into your bed."

Her eyes went wide, and gone was the shyness, replaced with hissing and spitting fire. Oh yeah, I liked that better.

But then, as quickly as she sparked, the flame went out,

the cool façade back into place. "I probably won't see you in the morning. I'm sure you'll be replaced by then."

I grinned at her. I went over and tossed myself on the couch. Damn, this thing was comfortable. And it was deep enough for my big body. "Sure thing. It was good to see you, butterfly."

"Hailey. My name is Hailey. You know my name."

I shook my head. "Nah, I prefer butterfly."

"You are impossible. God, I would be so happy not to see your smug face again."

"Are you sure about that? Because something tells me you'll miss me." I deliberately flashed my widest grin at her. The one that usually stunned people into submission.

I wasn't a complete idiot. I knew what I looked like. When I wasn't smiling, I looked as foreboding as any giant Viking probably would. But when I smiled, it always had the most interesting effect on people, women especially. I hadn't really understood it until I was about eleven or so. Every time I'd smiled, my mother had just shaken her head and then given me what I wanted.

When I got a little older and way more interested in girls,

all it really took was a smile. Then I'd grown a lot bigger, and that smile became even handier.

Unfortunately, the smile didn't exactly have the desired effect on Hailey. It just made her scowl.

Damn it. Was it broken?

I smiled even harder. She just rolled her eyes and stomped back to her room.

There was no way in hell I was letting any other guy replace me in her detail. She could request a replacement all she wanted, but she was stuck with me.

She just didn't know it yet.

CHAPTER SEVEN

Hailey

As soon as the alarm on my phone went off, I immediately reached over and tapped the screen to silence it. With a groan, I sat up and rubbed my eyes. I wasn't sure why I'd even bothered staying in bed this long.

It wasn't like I'd gotten much sleep.

There was a big, huge problem sleeping out in my living room, and I wouldn't rest until I'd corrected it.

Before I could do that, I needed to get myself together for the day. It was still too early to call Noah Blake and demand a replacement, although part of me wanted to disturb him after he'd messed up my peaceful life by sticking me with Oskar in the first place. Not that he was aware of that.

That was the problem with secrets. They could really screw up a good thing, and you couldn't even explain to anyone what the problem was.

I took a steaming hot shower, allowing the water to loosen the muscles that were tense after a long, sleepless night. Once I was out and dry, I took my hair down from its bun and fluffed the curls out. My skincare routine and makeup application were always the same, so I had it down to an exact science. Minimal foundation, mascara and perfectly sculpted brows. One swipe of my signature lipstick in a neutral mauve color and I was set.

It had been about an hour since I'd woken up, so I figured if Noah Blake wasn't awake yet, he was about to be. My cell phone didn't have his number programmed in, but I found it easily in the packet of information he'd provided me and my father with yesterday. The phone rang twice before a deep voice answered.

"Yes, Mr. Blake. This is Hailey Livingston."

"Miss Livingston. I trust everything is all right since the last check-in Oskar posted was an all-clear."

"Um, I didn't know anything about that. But no, everything is not all right. I need another.... person. Bodyguard. Whatever."

He paused for a beat, and I got the sense that I'd surprised him. Something I was sure didn't happen often.

"If Oskar has offended you in some way, I apologize. His jokes can be a bit off-color sometimes. I can have a talk with him."

Oh crap, now I felt bad. Despite not wanting Oskar anywhere near me, I genuinely was not trying to get him into trouble. Just because he was big, annoying, and frustratingly handsome, it didn't mean that I wanted to interfere in his career.

"He hasn't offended me. It's nothing like that." I sighed. There really wasn't any way to explain why I didn't want Oskar around unless I was willing to divulge our past. Clearly, Oskar hadn't told his boss that he'd picked me up on my birthday in Vegas and gotten me drunk and horny. If he hadn't said anything, then I wasn't going to either.

"It's more a personality-difference thing. Isn't there anyone else? Perhaps someone quiet and older? Much older."

Noah cleared his throat. "We're short-staffed right now so unfortunately, no. Let's give it a few days. Maybe things will work out by then."

I wasn't sure what he meant by that. Maybe we'd have assurances that I wasn't in any danger, or maybe I'd have murdered Oskar in his sleep by then?

"Okay. Thanks."

After we hung up, I took my time putting my earrings on. Just because Oskar was hanging around didn't mean that I had to acknowledge him. He was here for me, not the other way around. I would just ignore him and pretend he wasn't there.

When I walked out into the living room, Oskar turned around and my heart jumped into my throat. He wasn't wearing anything but a pair of sweatpants that hung scandalously low on his lean hips.

Stop staring.

My brain ignored that advice and continued a visual exploration of the ropy muscles that defined his chest and arms. How was it possible for any man to be that shredded? It really wasn't fair. No one could be expected to be strong under these circumstances.

Then I noticed what he was doing.

"You ate the last of my bread!"

He shrugged and looked down at the gluten-free toast in his hand. "I was hungry. What's so special about this bread anyway, other than the fact that it tastes like salty cardboard?"

I put my fingers to my temples.

"Look, we're stuck together for now. But I plan to call Noah soon, and then you'll be out on your ass."

Silently, I hoped that Noah hadn't already told him that I'd tried to get him replaced. Hopefully his boss wouldn't want to tell him that I wanted someone else. If he found out that Noah already rejected my request for a replacement, he'd be insufferable.

"Let's go."

He chewed loudly. "I'm not done with my salty cardboard."

"You are not going to interfere in my routine. You work for me."

Oskar winked. "I don't mind taking direction, butterfly. But then, you already knew that."

I spun around and stalked back to my room. The sounds of him moving around proved that at least he was taking me at my word and getting ready. Being late was completely unprofessional, and I worked hard to set a good example for the staff. Although having a man who looked like Oskar following me around at work probably wasn't setting the best example.

My father clearly hadn't thought this through. It wasn't like people wouldn't notice that I suddenly had a twenty-four-hour babysitter. It was more than a little strange and would probably draw more attention to me rather than less. I groaned.

Just thinking about spending the next eight hours cooped up in an office with Oskar was giving me claustrophobia. Maybe I could claim to be sick and just stay home. But as soon as I had the thought, I rejected it. He was not going to mess with my routine.

He'd messed with my emotions enough over the past few years.

When I opened the door and stepped out into the living room, I did a double take. Oskar was dressed in slim, black trousers that emphasized how muscular his legs were. His shirt wasn't collared but one of those jersey-knit types that hugged the body like a glove.

Bad idea. This was all a bad idea.

"That was fast. I expected to have to wait for you to shower."

He grinned. "Already showered before you even woke up, butterfly."

His insistence on using that nickname, even after I'd told him not to, made me grit my teeth. But telling him off again would only give him satisfaction, so I resolved to ignore him. I would think of him like one of those annoying little gnats that you couldn't catch so you pretended you couldn't see it.

"To the office, right?"

I nodded and then handed over my keys. His brow furrowed, but he accepted them in that massive hand of his.

"What's this?"

"Keys to the car. Since we're stuck together, I guess you're my chauffeur now." Then I turned and walked out without waiting to see if he was following.

I heard a door slam behind me before Oskar stepped into the elevator next to me.

"You know, this doesn't have to be difficult. I'm here to protect you, not piss you off."

"Pissing me off seems to be a natural by-product of protecting me."

"Sorry about that. I promised that this would be easy, and it will be. All you have to do is keep me in the loop about what you're doing so I can make sure it's safe, and then I'll stay out of your way."

When he put it like that, I felt a little petty. He was just trying to do his job, the same way I was. It wasn't his fault that we'd been thrown together, and despite how things ended between us after the weekend that we'd been together, we'd had a really good time. What more had I really been expecting? That the random guy I met in Vegas would be my one true love? That we'd ride off into the sunset on a white horse?

Even if Oskar hadn't snuck out the way he did, we still would have gone our separate ways afterward. So maybe he did me a favor. He'd rocked my world and then taught me why it was best not to trust random strangers. It was a life lesson that many people didn't learn until too late.

"You're right. We can be professional, do our jobs, and stay out of each other's way. I'll have you linked-in to my calendar so you'll know my schedule. And once my father is assured that I'm safe, he'll see that none of this is really necessary anyway. So really, it's just a temporary situation."

But as we rode the elevator down to the parking garage, I had the sinking feeling that nothing about this situation was temporary.

Oskar

After we reached the office, Hailey wasted no time settling in. Her secretary, an older woman with graying hair styled up into a high bun, brought her coffee and a small bowl of fruit, which she ate while staring at her computer.

There were two chairs in front of her desk, but my promise had been to be invisible, so I retreated to the couch on the other side of her office. She had a nice little setup, the coffee table and couch combination making it feel more like a small apartment than a sterile office.

Since Hailey was busy, I took the time to read my own emails.

Her assistant had already sent the calendar link, so I was able to review Hailey's upcoming schedule. After just looking at the first few days, I was tired on her behalf.

The woman in question stood and stretched before walking over to the windows. I watched, enjoying the view of her long legs in her pencil skirt and the wild fall of her hair over her shoulders. The past few years had been good to her. When we'd met, she'd been a beautiful girl who seemed a little unsure of herself with an endearing touch of vulnerability, and now she'd become a confident woman who could go toe-to-toe with anyone who got in her way.

Something I admired and found sexy as hell.

Hailey put one hand on the wall and then leaned back, stretching her back out. But the move also thrust her ass in the air, showcasing the full, round globes and the slender curve of her waist.

Yanking my eyes back to my phone, I tried to discreetly adjust the boner in my pants. Maybe these slacks had been a bad choice. I'd wanted to dress up a little to fit the environment, but I doubted having a tentpole in my pants all day would give off the conservative, corporate vibe.

That was how it went all day. Hailey ignored me and did a million small things that made all of the blood leave my brain. Meanwhile, I suffered in silence while checking in with Matthias on how her background check was going and praying for a miracle. Or a cold shower.

Ironically, the more I ignored Hailey, the more she seemed to want my attention. After her little yoga stretch this morning, I'd been determined to focus on anything but how she looked. Once I'd done some preliminary research on every event she had booked over the next few weeks, I looked up to notice her staring while sucking on the end of an ink pen.

When I didn't respond to that, Hailey got up and decided she needed to take a nap on the couch. The couch that I was currently sitting on. I didn't move fast enough, so she ended up almost lying on top of me. I probably left skid marks on the ground with how quickly I got up then. Hailey just huffed and then rolled over to sleep.

Rolled over and pointed her ass at me, I should say. Or at least that's what my dick saw.

Fuck.

I pulled out my phone to text Noah. It was time to find out who was relieving me, because I couldn't take any more.

That was when I saw I already had a text message from Dylan.

Dylan: Running a little late. Matthias wanted me to check on something first.

Oskar: Whatever it is, I'll do it for you if you just get here. Now.

Dylan: Did someone pee in your protein shake this morning? I thought you'd be happy protecting the Park Avenue Princess. Jonas said she was hot.

Oskar: Just get your ass here.

Ten minutes later, Dylan strolled in looking smug. Hailey was still asleep, so I didn't bother saying goodbye, but instead walked out. My phone chimed with a text.

Dylan: Dude, what the hell did she do to you?

I didn't bother to answer. I needed to go home, take a shower and jack off. In that order and probably several times.

By the time seven o'clock rolled around, I was ready. After a shower (okay, three showers), I felt more like myself. There was no telling what kind of weird magic spell

Hailey had cast on me that morning, but I was a consummate professional. I'd never treated a client inappropriately and wouldn't be starting now. Maybe she hadn't been aware of how she was torturing me this morning, or maybe this was her twisted form of revenge. Either way, I had to rise above it. Taking a breather in the afternoons was exactly what I needed. It gave me the chance to breathe air that didn't smell like Hailey and get a workout in.

Dylan had been texting me random updates all day, and I'd finally just put my phone on silent so I could concentrate. If I dropped a barbell on my foot because I was distracted, the guys would never let me hear the end of that.

Her calendar put the end of her workday at seven o'clock. When I arrived, Dylan put out his fist for a bump and then yelled, "Bye, Hailey!" over his shoulder.

She waved, and the happy smile on her face brought back my earlier annoyance. Dylan got smiles and waves, while I'd gotten scowls and the boner from hell.

Hailey's smile dropped as her eyes landed on me. She picked up her handbag from the floor by her desk, bending at the waist for an unnecessarily long time.

Hello, boner, my old friend.

I cursed as she finally straightened and stalked past me without a word but said a cheerful goodnight to her assistant.

Down in the parking garage, Hailey waited until I pointed out where I'd parked her car. The silence was almost as torturous as watching her sleep, so I opened the passenger door, trying to be nice.

She moved to the back door. "I'm sitting in the back."

With a sigh, I moved to open the back door. Hailey's eyes flared, clearly surprised at my easy acceptance of her brattiness. Truthfully, I was tired and about a half a second away from picking her gorgeous ass up and throwing her in the backseat. Anything that kept her out of my sight for a while would work.

There was only so long a guy could have a boner before risking permanent damage, right? Or at least that was what I remembered from all those commercials on TV late at night.

On the drive home, I thought about what excuse I could give Noah for needing to be transferred off this job. While we'd been friends for years, he wasn't an easy guy to get to know. It wasn't like we were hanging out over beers and telling each other our life stories. He was a hard-ass and didn't accept excuses, so unless I came down with an incurable illness over the next hour, I was probably stuck for at least a few weeks. Maybe I could bribe Dylan into switching with me more often, though. Hailey would probably be fine with that since they had seemed to hit it off.

Just one more thing to rub salt in the wound.

As I turned to head back to Hailey's building, a black sedan cut someone off as it turned the corner. New York drivers were wild, and no matter how long I lived here I'd never get used to that.

It was a short ride back to her place, but I turned on some music anyway. I turned the dial before settling on a country music station. Hailey's soft giggle lowered the tension in the car a bit. Hey, I liked songs about heartbreak and lost love.

At the next turn, I glanced in the side view mirror again. A black sedan. The same one that I'd seen ten minutes ago. What were the odds that same car would still be behind us?

Someone was following us.

My phone was in the cup holder next to me, so I used the voice commands to call Matthias. Luckily, I'd put my earpiece in before driving off, so I could have this conversation without Hailey overhearing all of it.

"Matthias. En route but have an unwelcome visitor. A black sedan. No visual on the driver."

I kept my voice down, hoping the music would cover half of what I was saying, but Hailey's head still popped up.

"Take the secondary route back to the office. I'll have Rafe waiting to cover you in case you're followed."

My eyes met Hailey's in the rearview briefly. I didn't think she really knew anything was wrong, which was how I wanted to keep it. Despite all her big talk about this being temporary and how she didn't need security, I saw the look on her face this morning in the elevator. She was worried even if she didn't want to be.

The car on the right sped up and weaved around a truck until there was only one car between us. Shit. He wasn't just following us. Clearly, he had some intention to engage because no one would get this close if their goal was not to be noticed. My hands tightened on the wheel as I glanced at Hailey in the rearview again. She was wearing her seatbelt, but I was regretting my decision to allow her to sit in the back alone.

Chauffeur jokes aside, if this guy hit us, Hailey was right in the strike zone.

"Hailey, I don't want to scare you. But there's a car following us, and I'm concerned that he might try to run us off the road. I need you to hang on."

"What? Someone's following us?" Hailey's terrified eyes were the last thing I saw before something rammed us from behind.

"Oskar!"

I struggled to keep the wheel straight as the car fishtailed. Horns blared next to me, and I hit the gas, weaving around a slow minivan. The light ahead was yellow, but I was going to have to run it. If I stopped, that was giving whoever was following us an opportunity to get to Hailey. Something I couldn't allow.

The next blow came from the left side. The sedan was right behind us now, and there was a loud screech of metal as he connected with our bumper.

"Oh my God. What are we going to do?" Hailey screamed

again at the next blow, and hearing the terror in her voice spurred me into action.

I wrenched the wheel to the right, forcing the car into a spin. As we looped around, I sent up a silent prayer there were no pedestrians nearby, since I had no control of the car. For a moment, I thought the maneuver had worked and the black sedan wouldn't have the room to execute such a tight turn.

But as soon as our car stopped moving, I looked up to see it barreling toward us and realized I'd made a grave error. I'd thought his intent was to scare us, but it was pretty clear the intent was to kill.

And my mistake was going to cost us. I hit the gas but not fast enough, and the last sound I heard before the crash was Hailey's terrified scream.

CHAPTER EIGHT

Hailey

I adjusted the ice pack on my temple and shivered. Because I'd been belted in during the crash, I hadn't sustained any real damage, but damned if the bump on my head didn't hurt.

"Here's some coffee. Is there anything else I can get you?"

Jonas had been so nice since I arrived, making sure I had an ice pack and offering me food and even a bed to rest in until their private physician arrived. They'd given me the choice of going to the hospital, but once I found out they had a private doctor on call, I was more than happy to go that route. My family wasn't usually tabloid fodder, but with the launch of the new fragrance line coming up, I wanted to keep the focus where it should be—the perfume —and not on whether or not someone was trying to kill me.

Plus, it wasn't going to be easy to reassure my father as it was, much less if he had to visit me in the hospital.

"No, this is perfect. Thank you." I was interrupted by a shiver that wracked my body so hard I almost dropped the mug of coffee. "I still can't believe it happened. It's hard to believe that someone out there wants me dead."

"Our team is the best, and we will find out who is doing this. Has anything happened out of the ordinary lately? I hate to ask but anything you can remember might be helpful."

Instead of brushing it off and saying *of course not* the way I had originally, I took a minute to really think. It was impossible to run a division of a company without pissing someone off. I had exacting standards and expected everyone who worked for me to do their jobs and do them well. But that was just business. Nothing that I had done was any different than any other boss in a corporate position.

Why would someone want to kill me because of that?

"I'm pretty boring. All I do is go to work and then go straight home. But it's hard to imagine anyone I know at work doing something like this. Most of our employees have been with us for years."

"Well, if it is someone from work, Matthias will find it. No one can hide from him." Jonas left me with one last, sympathetic smile.

As soon as he left, someone sat on the couch right next to me. It was Noah's wife, who I'd been introduced to earlier.

Lucia was a pretty, petite brunette with soft gray eyes and hair that was almost as curly as mine. She was the exact opposite of the type of woman I'd expected to be married to such an intense man, but it had only taken thirty seconds of seeing them together to understand why they made sense. She was his perfect counterpart in every way and softened his rough edges. He also couldn't keep his eyes off her.

Must be nice.

I sighed. Jealousy wasn't helping my headache.

"The doctor should be here soon. He's really nice and he'll take good care of you."

"Thank you, Lucia. You've been very kind. I'm sure this is

an imposition having some banged-up girl hanging out here for hours."

She chuckled and took a sip of the mug of tea she'd put on the coffee table in front of us.

"It's no problem. There's too much testosterone around here anyway."

"Girl, say it louder for the people in the back." A blond woman with her hair in a high ponytail plopped down on the couch next to Lucia. "But there are benefits to that. Especially in the morning when they're all in the gym. Holy abdominals."

Lucia covered her mouth with her hand. "Don't let Jonas hear you say that. The last time he caught you drooling over Oskar shirtless, he was pouting for a week."

JJ's eyes swung my way. "Speaking of our own resident He-Man, I heard Oskar is the one guarding you."

I adjusted the ice pack again, wishing I could drop it down my cleavage to cool off some. Thinking about Oskar was the last thing I needed right now. After the crash, he'd been like a superhero. The car that'd chased us had sped away, but he'd gotten out of the car like some kind of avenging angel, putting himself between me and potential harm.

Luckily, I wasn't hurt too badly, just a bump on the head, but he'd insisted on lifting me out of the car anyway. The ambulance and police had arrived shortly after, and he'd handled everything so I didn't have to. I could tell the EMTs weren't thrilled that I refused further medical treatment, but I hadn't wanted to be separated from Oskar right then.

Maybe it was the minor head injury but all the animosity I'd felt toward him all day had melted away instantly when I saw how concerned he was for me.

"Oskar has been great. I'm not sure what I would have done if some crazy person had chased me when I was on my own. The accident definitely would have been a lot worse."

JJ nodded slowly. "Yes, mmm hmm. That's all well and good, but I was talking about those guns. Have you seen his arms? He looks like he could bench press this building."

Lucia rolled her eyes. "Sorry about her. We've tried training her; it never works. The most important thing is that Oskar got you here as fast as possible. You'll be safe here."

JJ crossed her arms. "I wasn't saying safety isn't important. Geez, Lu. You act like I'm some monster."

Lucia frowned. "I'm sorry, JJ. I didn't mean it like that."

I tensed as I glanced between the two friends. JJ looked really hurt and upset. These two had clearly known each other a long time, something I was envious of. My friends from college were scattered all over the country, and I would have loved to have my best friend living so close.

Suddenly JJ broke into a huge grin and patted her friend's arm. "Damn, Lucia. You're so easy, every time."

"Ugh! I should have known." But Lucia was smiling as she sat back against the couch.

JJ turned to me. "Seriously though, everything really will be okay. These guys are the best."

Not that I needed any more convincing after watching Oskar in action earlier, but her words still managed to comfort me. Everything seemed like it was suddenly moving so fast. One minute I'd been reconsidering the idea of having private security, and the next I was almost run off the road by a madman.

How had my comfortable, orderly life gone so haywire in just a few days?

"Thank you. I needed to hear that. Even though I didn't think I needed protection at first, I'm grateful for it now."

"You won't regret hiring Blake Security. Besides, even though this scary thing is happening, you get to enjoy one amazing perk." JJ waggled her eyebrows suggestively. "While under protection, you get to spend all that time with our very own modern-day Viking."

We all laughed, but I could only hope my blush wasn't visible. These women knew Oskar, the man that he was today, not the irresponsible, carefree version of him that I'd known briefly years ago. He was their friend and a respected colleague. They could joke about how hot he was in a casual way, and it was no big deal. But for me, it was impossible to view him as just another hot guy. He was THE hot guy, the one who had rocked my world and left me reeling and aching for more.

No, there was nothing funny about the way Oskar made me feel.

"That's definitely a perk," I conceded, unable to resist laughing along with them. Even if thoughts of him made me feel like I was on the verge of self-destructing, that wasn't their fault.

I mean, they all lived together. So despite their dirty laughs, they probably thought of the guy as family, considering that he'd worked for Blake Security so long.

JJ leaned forward suddenly. "Have you seen him naked yet? I bet that dude has a battle ax hanging between his legs, doesn't he?"

Having just taken a sip of my tea, I choked slightly, sending them into another fit of laughter.

Okay, clearly they didn't think of him as family.

***

Oskar

As image after image flashed on the screen in front of me, my rage only grew. How was it possible to have this much video footage and not one clear shot of the asshole who'd crashed into us?

Matthias held up his hands as my eyes shifted over to him. "I know, man. Trust me, I know. I've combed all the surveillance available from the businesses in the area, and somehow this asshole managed to always be just out of range or coincidentally turning his head away. Bastard got lucky."

"Or he's really fucking good." I dropped a fist down on the conference table, relishing the pain in my knuckles as we watched the footage again.

After the accident, my body had gone into overdrive. We were all trained in evasive maneuvers and basic first aid, but I'd been on a rampage at just the thought that someone might hurt Hailey.

I was sure I'd scared her a little with my intensity, but all I'd been able to think was that I'd put her in danger. Again. Seeing her bruised and with blood on her face had not only frozen me with fear but also triggered the guilt I'd been trying to outrun for years. She was supposed to be safe and protected. It was the entire reason I'd run from her the first time.

Now she was in danger all over again and this time, the solution wasn't as simple as getting on a plane.

"He'll make a mistake eventually. They all do. And when he does, I'll be there." Matthias narrowed his eyes as we came to the last still image he'd captured from the video surveillance.

It was a grainy, blurred picture of the man who'd been driving the car. There wasn't much detail, so all we knew was it was a white male with dark hair and seemingly average build.

Which could easily describe any random guy on the streets of New York.

Hell, I couldn't even explain how the guy had known where we'd be. Hailey usually left work around the same time each day, but we'd made sure to use different routes when driving her. Yet this guy had no problem following us.

The faint sound of laughter trickled in behind us. I turned around to see Hailey laughing with Lucia. Seeing her so happy and carefree brought up a longing so acute that I ached with it. This was how she should always be. I was grateful to Lucia for making her feel so welcome, something that I hadn't been able to accomplish.

I hung my head. This guy was going to get away with it and the knowledge burned in my gut. How could I protect Hailey with so little information? Based on what she'd told us, she didn't interact with others enough to have many potential enemies. Her life was her company, and that was it. This should have been the easiest case to crack, yet we'd been two steps behind this guy the whole time.

All she wanted was to focus on her work, and I couldn't give her that. It was a difficult thing when all I wanted was to give her everything.

I'd failed her once again.

When I turned around, Matthias was watching me. His eyes darted behind me to where the women were sitting.

I'd been stupid to think that my interest in Hailey would go unnoticed much longer. People think women gossip, but this merry band of killers I lived with were like a bunch of old hens when it came to gossip. They couldn't resist asking the questions that you didn't want to answer, and we all knew way too much about each other's business around here.

"What's going on with you?" Matthias finally said. "And don't say nothing because I've seen you with this girl and it's definitely something."

I shook my head. "She's my charge, and she just got hurt in a car accident that I should have been able to prevent. That's something."

He closed his laptop, and the video feed he'd projected

onto the wall disappeared. "It's more than that. But you don't have to tell me anything. Just be careful."

"Careful of what?"

He laughed. "Don't you see who she's talking to out there?"

"She was talking to Lucia." I turned around, my eyes immediately going to Hailey.

No matter where we were or how many other people were around, she always drew my attention first, like she was the only star in my sky. Under different circumstances, maybe I'd want to investigate what that meant, but right now the only thing that mattered was keeping her safe.

Lucia moved slightly and then I saw who was sitting next to her. I cursed under my breath.

"Yeah, JJ is probably out there spilling all your dirty secrets right now." Matthias looked like he was enjoying that idea way too much.

"I doubt she's spilling any secrets, but that doesn't mean she isn't going to embarrass the hell out of me anyway."

He shrugged. "That's generally JJ's goal in life."

We both turned to watch the women again. Hailey fit in

with the other two as if she belonged. Maybe this was a good thing. If she had friends here, then it would be easier to convince her to spend more time at headquarters. At least here, I could guarantee her safety. Surrounded by a team of trained former assassins and a former cop, there was nowhere safer in New York City.

And in that moment, I knew what I needed to do.

"I need to bring her here. That's the only way to keep her safe."

Matthias snorted. "Good luck getting her to agree to that."

"Yeah, no kidding."

It was no secret around the office that Hailey hadn't wanted security. And she'd given the guys even more material to use against me when she'd requested a replacement bodyguard the next day. Since I hadn't said anything to her about it, she probably thought Noah hadn't told me about her request. I chuckled. She clearly didn't know how guys thought. Noah had not only told me but the rest of the team as well, who'd taken great delight in messing with me.

Especially since she'd had no problem with Dylan on his shifts.

"I don't like how many blank holes there are in this case. This guy is good, and he seems able to pop up out of nowhere. This is the only place she'll be completely safe until we figure this shit out."

Matthias nodded. "Not disagreeing with you. But are you ready for the fight you're about to have on your hands when you ask her to move here?"

Although I winced a little at the thought—Hailey was a bit of a hellcat when she didn't get her way—I was already formulating a plan of attack.

"Don't worry about me. I've got this covered. I know exactly how to handle Hailey."

Matthias looked skeptical. "Really? How's that?"

I shrugged. "I'm not going to give her a choice."

CHAPTER NINE

Hailey

Why had I agreed to this again?

Because somebody tried to run you off the road. That's three times now. First, your apartment, then the boutique, and now this. Maybe it's time to stop being stubborn.

I wasn't being stubborn. I just needed my life to work right. And honestly, I wasn't that interesting. I had no idea why someone would want to hurt me. But there I was, sitting in my apartment with a mild headache while Oskar packed clothes for me.

The last thing on earth that I wanted to do was go back to a penthouse full of people.

Relax. The place is so big you'll probably never even see anyone.

Yes, that was a good point, but still. I liked my privacy. I liked things *just so*. With that many people milling about, someone would surely notice my OCD tendencies.

I glanced up. One of the young guys was at the door. His posture was relaxed, but his gaze was watchful.

When he saw I was assessing him, he gave me a wide smile. "Do you need anything?"

I shook my head. "Um, no, thank you."

This was my house. Shouldn't I be offering him something? "I mean, I guess I live here, so do *you* want a drink or something?"

His grin was easy. "No, I'm good. Don't worry. Relax. You'll be okay."

Like Oskar, his smile completely changed his face. When he smiled he could easily have been a cover model for a magazine. Who was I kidding? Most of those guys could be cover models. With their easy swagger and well, let's face it, chiseled jawlines, I wasn't immune. I did have working female parts, and those parts noticed exactly how handsome every single one of those men from Blake Security was.

Seriously, did Noah Blake run some kind of hot-model bodyguard agency? Even the women were gorgeous. It was slightly intimidating to be completely honest.

Oskar came out of the bedroom with a couple of bags and the pink zippered pouch I used for my toiletries.

I couldn't move. I couldn't even think. How had this become my life?

It wasn't until an hour later when we were in the car on our way to Blake Security that I even bothered to look inside the duffel Oskar had packed for me. I reached in and felt something silky. I frowned. Was that a—

"You packed lingerie?"

Heat sneaked up my neck as I looked around to see who was in the backseat. No one. Where had Dylan gone? I'd been so out of it, I hadn't even paid attention.

"Relax. I packed the essentials."

He missed nothing though, and added softly, "Dylan is in

the follow car. You're okay. We have you."

Having people look over my shoulder all the time was wearing on my nerves in a way I hadn't even known was possible.

"Are you insane? That's the problem, isn't it? All this time I've been responding as if dealing with a sane person. I should have modified my behavior for someone completely bonkers."

"You think I'm crazy?"

"Oh, undoubtedly. That would also explain how and why you vanished on me back then. Someone locked you in an insane asylum."

Oskar snickered. "Not exactly. And you can relax. I brought extra clothes. Even though you do look better in my shirts. Your 'less fun' clothes are in the trunk."

I flushed again, remembering that day in the hotel when he had finally let me get dressed so we could eat on the balcony. I wore one of his shirts and a pair of long socks so my feet didn't get cold, even though it was the dead of summer. Due to my poor circulation, I was always chilled. Something he'd learned very quickly.

"You're impossible."

"Weirdly enough, you're not the first person to ever tell me that."

"How long am I going to be trapped at Blake Security?"

His gaze went serious then. In moments like that when his expression was grim, he looked more like the pillaging marauder I'd expected when I first met him.

"Until we catch the motherfucker trying to kill you. Until then, you'll be kept safe."

I gave him a wan smile. "Yup, in my gilded tower. This is going to be a long stretch, isn't it?"

"Well, look at it this way. At least the scenery is going to be hot."

***

Oskar

So far, she hadn't smiled, but she hadn't scowled either... so I'd take that as a win. "Okay, this is your room."

When I realized she was going to be staying, I'd asked Lucia to help me add some flowers and change out the blinds and curtains. The room was already well decorated just like she liked, contemporary and stuff, I guess. But I wanted to make it... prettier somehow. Softer. God, I hoped she'd like it.

You are such a sap. It doesn't matter if she likes it. She's not here to critique your interior design.

No, she wasn't. She was here so we could protect her. That was all that really mattered, but I still wanted her to be comfortable.

"Bathroom is over here. It's got a soaking tub, you know, if you want to take a bath or something."

"This is more like a swimming pool."

I grinned. "Well, I'm a big guy."

"You take baths?" Her brows lifted, and her lips twisted into a sardonic smirk.

"I find them very relaxing. Enough with the judgy eyes. Grab a shower. It's got a rainwater shower, but you can adjust it here." I showed her where to change from the rain shower into a regular shower. "Then you can take a regular shower with the nozzle. I remember you telling me that rain showers are the enemy of every curly-haired woman in the world."

She blinked rapidly. "You remember that?"

I swallowed as the heat rushed up my neck and, I was pretty certain, into my face. "Yeah, no big deal. I remember lots of stuff."

"That's um... thoughtful."

I nodded. "Yeah, so I know you brought your own stuff, but these toiletries are pretty good, too. Noah sources from the same place that some hotel in Dubai uses. Especially that lotion. It makes your skin soft."

Why did you say that? Stop talking. Stop talking right now.

"I will keep that in mind, I guess."

She followed me back out into the bedroom. "The closet is over there. It's a walk-in. We didn't bring much, but we'll send someone to get the rest of your stuff."

"Just how long do you think I'll be staying?"

I shrugged. "A while... I don't know honestly."

"Well, I won't be staying that long."

"Great. Then you won't need the closet. But just in case you do, it's here and there is more than enough room."

She swallowed hard, a line of worry creasing her forehead. I wanted to kiss it away.

What is wrong with you?

I cleared my throat. "Obviously, this is the bed."

"Yeah, obviously. It's huge."

I refrained from making any more *well, I'm a huge guy* kind of comments. That really wasn't going to help.

Look at you, showing restraint.

The door was open, and I could hear Jonas and JJ hanging out in the living room. I hoped they didn't keep her up at night. Those two were loud, especially JJ.

"This is amazing. Thank you. I appreciate it. The room is nice."

"Of course, this is the nicest room. No other suitable guest rooms were available anyway." Liar. In reality, I just wanted her in my space.

Jonas's voice was loud and clear. "What are you talking about? There are like five other open guest rooms in here."

Fucking hell.

"Um, what I meant was—"

JJ, of course, had to chime in. "Sorry to cock block!"

Honestly, I was going to kill them.

Hailey blinked. "This is *your* room?"

I nodded. "Yeah, it's mine, but the other rooms aren't as comfortable. There are no modifications for the shower and the tub, so I figured you'd like it better in here."

Like the sad sap you are, you just wanted her in your space.

Yeah, that too.

"So where are you sleeping?" Hailey asked.

My inner asshole laughed. *Yeah big guy, where are you sleeping?*

"I'm actually already in the guest room next door. If you need anything, just knock on the door and I'll get it for you."

"Now I feel bad that I've put you out of your room."

"Don't feel bad. Like I said, the guest rooms don't have any nice amenities."

She shifted on her feet and tugged on the hem of her blouse. "I—I don't know what to say. Thank you hardly seems like enough."

"It's enough. And you don't need to thank us. Your father, your company, hired us to do a job, and we're going to do it. We'll keep you safe. Forget about the threat for now, okay? You don't have to be afraid of anything here."

She nodded. "Okay, then in that case, thank you for doing such a great job."

"Don't mention it."

A few moments passed with us staring at each other uncertainly. I don't know how I found the strength to stay still because all I wanted to do was march straight to her, gather her in my arms and tell her I would kill anything that tried to hurt her.

Instead, I pushed away from the dresser. "Right, I guess I should go. Unless you need anything else?"

She glanced over at the bed and I struggled to keep my eyes straight ahead. Hailey probably wasn't even aware of how much she telegraphed with her face. But everything she was thinking was all there in her eyes. The want, the longing and the fear.

If she said she needed me, walking away would be damn near impossible and the hardest thing I'd had to do in years.

CHAPTER TEN

Hailey

Being alone in a room with Oskar was a recipe for trouble, so I decided it was time to explore the rest of my new living space. Hopefully a little distance would help me to stop imagining him spread out across that king size bed.

I could feel Oskar following me as I walked down the hall and back to the waiting area where I'd spent the most time. The living room to the right of that looked comfortable and inviting. It had clearly once been an industrial space but I could tell someone had put a lot of time and effort into making it a home.

The thought of Noah Blake picking out pillows and knick-knacks made me laugh a little. What I was seeing was no doubt his wife's influence. I was sure all the men who lived there couldn't care less if they had comfortable furniture and throw pillows.

"We can hang out and watch a movie later if you want." Oskar pointed out the television hanging on the wall. Below it was a console table and I could see a game system and controllers on top.

"Sure. That sounds fun. I'm a little hungry right now though."

Oskar blinked. "Right. I need to feed you." He took my elbow and led me around the corner to the kitchen.

It was a little strange that he was treating me like an exotic pet that he was responsible for. I didn't like it. He didn't need to feed me; I was more than capable of doing that myself.

Not lately, you aren't.

My annoying inner voice reminded me that my efforts to take care of myself lately had been massive fails. All I had to show for my efforts was a big, empty penthouse and waning friendships. My best friend, Priya, kept telling me that I was going to grow cobwebs between my legs if I didn't put myself out there more.

Suddenly I missed her. A lot.

"Hey, what's wrong?" Oskar stopped his march toward the kitchen, peering at me with concern.

"Is everything okay?" Lucia's voice came from behind us.

I spun around and took a small step back. Oskar had me so distracted I hadn't realized that we were right on the edge of the kitchen. JJ and Lucia were at the huge island collecting plates and wiping down the counter.

"Oh, hi. I was just coming to get something to eat."

Lucia dropped the dishrag she was holding. "Oh no! If I'd known you guys were coming, we would have waited for you."

JJ rolled her eyes. "I don't think she wants any chicken surprise casserole, Lu."

I glanced over at Oskar. "And what is chicken surprise casserole?"

He shrugged sheepishly. "It's what Noah makes when it's

his turn to cook. He throws in chicken, vegetables and cheese. The surprise is whether or not he burns the fucking place down."

His deadpan humor was exactly what I needed just then. Everything was changing in my life, and it was starting to make me feel like I was on some rollercoaster, two shakes away from losing my lunch. But this was familiar, joking around with Oskar and allowing him to distract me from my problems.

It was a pattern with the two of us, going back to when we'd met. I'd been lonely and depressed, celebrating my twenty-first birthday alone. He'd made me feel better then, too.

I could only hope I'd learned my lesson and wouldn't allow my heart to get involved this time.

"It actually came out pretty tasty this time. Probably because he dumped a whole bag of cheese in there. We would have saved you some, but Dylan ate all the leftovers!" JJ gave the man in question a playful shove.

"Hey, I'm a growing boy."

I peeked over at him, amused. Dylan was nowhere near a boy. He might not be as buff as Oskar or as intense as Rafe and Noah, but he had an earnest, good-guy kind of appeal that reminded me of the actor who played Captain America.

The kind of guy you could take home to your parents but who would secretly do dirty things to you under the table when no one was looking.

"Well, I was going to make something, but I don't want to mess up the kitchen after you've already cleaned it."

Lucia waved that away. "Don't worry about that. Make yourself at home. If you want to cook, feel free."

"If you need a taste tester, I'm available." Dylan grinned over at me.

Oskar suddenly pushed past, blocking my view of the others. "Keep your tongue in your mouth. She doesn't need you tasting anything of hers."

The others hooted at that, and I could feel my cheeks burning. I ignored Oskar's knowing look and turned to survey what I had to use. The kitchen was a chef's dream with a double range and a massive island to work on. I was excited to have people to cook for, even if it was just me and Oskar and Dylan begging for scraps. Usually I had to heat up whatever my chef had left for me and eat alone.

Having a private chef was an amazing luxury, for sure, but there was something special about preparing food with your own hands for people to enjoy. It was definitely something I'd missed once I moved into the penthouse on my own.

My parents drove me crazy, but it had been fun to try different recipes when I was at home and know that there would always be someone around to share it with.

After careful consideration, I decided to make a quick frittata using some eggs and ham I'd found. It was quick and easy and would be done in about twenty minutes. Oskar perched on one of the bar stools, watching me as I puttered around the kitchen. I whisked the eggs and then added sour cream and cheese. A low grumble from Oskar made me drop the whisk.

"Sorry. It just looks really good. I'm starving." He smiled a slow, panty-melting grin at my response.

I turned my back on him and concentrated on the food. The cast iron skillet sizzled as I dropped in a generous amount of butter. Resolved to pay close attention so I didn't burn anything, I did my best to ignore Oskar's extremely obvious presence behind me, although it wasn't easy. The man seemed to have no idea how to sit quietly and instead spent the time offering his opinion on what I was cooking, suggesting what I should cook next time, and asking when it would be done. Luckily, it cooked up fast once I took the skillet from the stovetop to the oven.

"Can you grab some plates?" Maybe if I gave him something to do it would be easier to ignore how happy it made me to share a meal with him.

Five minutes later, we sat down to a steaming, cheesy vision.

"Seriously, this looks amazing. I'm not even sure what it is, but I can get down with fancy-ass scrambled eggs."

"It's frittata. It's baked eggs, cheese, ham and usually I throw in bacon too, but I didn't want it to take any longer than necessary."

Oskar took a huge bite and then paused. After a long moment, he gulped the food down, but it was obviously difficult.

"What? Is something wrong with it?" Hurriedly, I took a bite of my own and almost spit it out. "Great. I left out the salt, pepper and the garlic. I suck today."

"No, it's not bad. Look—" Oskar took another bite, and I

almost laughed as he struggled to keep his face neutral while he chewed.

I stood and picked up both plates. "No way am I going to let you eat this. Friends don't let friends eat bad food."

His chuckle followed me into the kitchen. I had seen sandwich fixings in the fridge earlier, so a turkey and cheese would have to do. While I pulled out the meat and cheese, Oskar disappeared into the walk-in pantry and came back with a loaf of bread.

"Sandwiches are one of my staple foods."

I appreciated that he wasn't making a big deal out of me ruining dinner. Or that the reason I'd ruined it was because I was so distracted by him. Or more specifically, by the sexy as hell sounds he made.

By the time we finished making our sandwiches, it was quiet in the penthouse. The lights were out in the main living area, and I could hear voices but only distantly.

Oskar must have seen my curiosity because he pointed to the hallway we'd come from. "My room is right next to Matthias and Gemma. Rafe and his wife are downstairs, too. Jonas and JJ are upstairs on the same level with Noah and Lucia."

I took another bite of my sandwich as I thought about the unique accommodations. It was a little strange, in my opinion, to live where you worked. There was no way I'd want to pull out a pillow in my office at Livingston. If I couldn't escape the work stress and go back to my quiet space and relax, I'd probably have an ulcer by now.

"What do you do when you just want to be alone?" I whispered, not wanting anyone to overhear us.

Just the fact that I felt compelled to whisper was a problem. I couldn't live in a place long-term where I felt like every word I said could be overheard.

Oskar finished the last bite of his sandwich, chewing noisily. "Everyone here is pretty cool. We respect each other and give each other space. Plus, we're all trained fighters. Not the kind of people you'd want to bother, you know? If I went to Matthias's room after hours, he'd open the door with a dagger at my throat. Hell, his wife probably would too."

"Wow. I guess I won't go exploring then." We laughed together as we cleaned up the mess we'd made and put all the food away.

"No, it's not like that. Plus, you don't have to worry about running into anyone after hours now. Everyone here is all married and boring now, so they're all in bed by like ten thirty at night."

We both startled when JJ stuck her head around the door into the kitchen. "Goodnight, Hailey!"

Then she grinned at Oskar and put up her middle finger. "And we go to bed early because we're *boning,* jackass."

I cracked up. "I have a feeling it's never a dull moment around here."

Oskar

Now that everyone had cleared out, it was so quiet it was almost eerie. I followed Hailey into the living room. I was glad she hadn't suggested going back to the bedroom yet. It was going to be a real challenge to sleep knowing that she was just down the hall in my room, surrounded by my scent.

Clearly, I was a glutton for punishment since there were two guestrooms open that I could have put her in. But no. I'd wanted her in my space, surrounded by my things. It did something to me seeing her in there.

Something that was only going to make it harder to let her go again when this was all over.

Hailey sat on one end of the couch and pulled her knees up to her chest. "I'm not sleepy yet. Do you think we could watch a movie now?"

I picked up the remote from the side table. When the TV turned on, it was still signed in to Netflix, so I gave her the remote so she could do a little channel surfing. Even though she seemed to be handling the sudden address change well so far, she also had the prickliness that was usually a precursor to a client losing their shit.

Most people underestimated how hard it was to allow someone else to judge what was safe for you. Hailey was fiercely independent, so having someone else coming in to upend her life had to be traumatic.

I took a seat on the couch next to her, leaving plenty of space between us. Hailey finally settled on an episode of some drama that I'd never seen before. After the first five minutes, I'd already given up on paying attention, mostly because Hailey had squirmed her way across the couch and was now cuddled up on my arm.

The scent of her wrapped around me, and for the first time all day I let out a breath of relief. It was probably a bad idea to spend time hanging out with her, but you couldn't have moved me just then with a crowbar.

Hailey laughed suddenly, and I glanced down at her. She froze when our eyes connected. Then her hand reached up and touched my cheek.

Kissing her would be a bad idea. I was ashamed to say that I had the thought and still did it anyway. Because in that moment, I wasn't thinking about the future or the past, only the two of us and how much I wanted her.

Hailey made a soft whimpering sound that went straight to my dick before climbing in my lap. If it was bad before when she was just sitting next to me, it was a million times worse to have all her curvy softness in my lap, her breasts rubbing against my chest. She wasn't trying to go anywhere, but I put one hand gently on the back of her head to hold her in place, relishing the soft wildness of her curls flowing over my fingers.

"Oh my God," she whispered when my lips migrated down to her ear.

The last time I'd heard that sound, we'd been in a Vegas suite, tangled in the sheets and sweaty after several rounds of lovemaking. It was like being suspended in time, caught between then and now, because the fire between us was still there.

Any thoughts I'd had about just being friends or moving on from the past were immediately turned to ashes against the sparks flying between us.

"Take this off." Hailey fumbled with the edge of my T-shirt, tugging it upward, but it was caught on my arms since I was still holding her.

All she could see and access was my torso, but that seemed to be enough to occupy her as her lips made their way down my neck and then skipped over the fabric to land on one of my exposed nipples.

"Ah, holy shit."

Her giggle vibrated over my skin, sending another wave of sensation that followed the amazing feeling of her little tongue lashing a path down toward...

"Wait. Shit, we can't do this."

Hailey groaned, her mouth still busy hovering right over the waistband of my pants. "But I want to. I don't want to be alone tonight. I'm tired of being alone."

The alpha male inside me roared at her words, ready to

throw her over my shoulder caveman style and spend the rest of the night inside her. But despite what everyone seemed to think of me, I was capable of more than just kicking ass and making dirty jokes.

"I guess I shouldn't be surprised. At least this time you didn't leave me to wake up the morning after wondering what I did wrong."

"Hailey. It wasn't like that."

"What was it like then? Because I remember it pretty well. And it sucked. You really hurt me, Oskar."

The hurt in her voice and in her eyes killed me. I'd never wished more that I could go back and change the past. And not just what had happened between us, but all the bad decisions I'd made prior to that which had caused me to be a danger to her.

"I'm so sorry about that. But there were things going on that I didn't want to touch you. Bad things. I haven't always been a good person, baby."

"I can't pretend I understand what you mean about bad things. But if you had to leave to keep me safe and to keep yourself safe, then I forgive you."

"You shouldn't. I don't deserve a girl like you, Hailey."

"Why would you say that?"

"Being with a guy like me would only put you in danger. And I never want to do to you what my father did to my mother. Being with him made her a target to his enemies. He put us all in danger, and it was fucked."

She looked surprised, but then she did the last thing I expected. She hugged me. Her arms wrapped around my back and squeezed.

The rush of emotion caught me off guard. It wasn't like I'd never been hugged before. Our crazy gang was probably more touchy-feely than most with lots of handshakes, bro hugs, and pounds on the back. Lucia in particular was prone to random bouts of affection, more than her husband appreciated.

But this was different. For the first time in a long time, I felt like I wasn't just an afterthought, or loved because of my relation to someone else. I was cared about as a part of Blake Security and that was great, but with Hailey, she cared about me for me. It wasn't because of my job or anything else.

She just cared for me. And it healed something inside me that I didn't even know was broken.

"I'm sorry about what happened to your mom. I'm sure your father didn't mean to put any of you in danger," Hailey whispered.

Still reeling from the onslaught of emotion her hug had caused, I knew that I needed to put some distance between us. She had a way of not only breaking down my walls but preventing me from putting up new ones.

"He didn't care enough to keep us safe. If he'd really loved us, he'd have stayed away. That's why I'll never get married. The best way to tell a woman I love her is to stay away from her."

She looked stricken. But I didn't soften my words or hold her close. It was time for this thing between us, whatever it was, to end.

"I'm going to my room now. If you need anything, just text me."

Hailey looked defeated but nodded. "I'm sorry for asking so many questions. I didn't mean to bring up bad memories."

"I shouldn't have told you all that stuff."

"Why not? We're friends, aren't we?"

"No, Hailey. We aren't friends. This thing tonight, it should have never happened. And it can't happen again. This is over."

Even though I meant every word, the hurt look in her eyes followed me as I left the room.

This was going to be a long night.

CHAPTER ELEVEN

Hailey

I chewed on the end of my pen, not hearing anything going on around me. It was the middle of the afternoon, and I should have been completely invested in this project-update meeting. But instead, the scene from the day before yesterday was playing over and over again in my head.

This is over.

Not exactly what any girl wanted to hear after a hot make-out session, right?

Apparently, he'd meant it too, since one of the other

guards had taken me to work yesterday and Dylan had come for me today.

Someone passed by on my right, and I snapped to attention. Jerry, one of our top scientists, was doing a presentation on the newest sample fragrances his team had been working on. I needed to get all this stuff with Oskar out of my head so I could focus.

Everything was almost ready for the launch of my signature perfume honoring my mother, but that wasn't the only thing on my plate. As Vice President of Product Development, I always needed to be a hundred steps ahead of our production schedule. Crafting the perfect fragrance took time, testing, tweaking and agonizing. Lots of agonizing on my part because I wouldn't approve any perfume unless I was sure it was absolutely perfect.

This was my domain. I was fantastic at my job and always in complete control. Some stupid squabble with a guy who wasn't even my boyfriend was not going to throw me off.

Except it was throwing me off, damn it. My shoulders sagged as Jerry sat down, and I realized I hadn't heard anything he'd said. I was completely off my game, and it was entirely due to one big, sexy, overgrown Viking.

"Excellent work, everyone." I forced myself to smile and

look alive as we all filed out of the conference room to go back to our desks.

My people worked hard, and I didn't want my personal life to impact anyone here. I'd always kept those two areas of my life separate for good reason, and I'd never questioned it before. The only reason I was suddenly unsure about things was Oskar forcing his way into my life and reminding me of everything I'd been missing.

Bastard.

"What did you think, Hailey? That this would end with a happily ever after and he'd marry you? Yeah right."

"Still mumbling to yourself, I see. Speak up, Hailey."

I almost stumbled over the doorjamb to my office at the sound of my mother's voice. "Mom! I didn't know you were coming in today. I would have postponed the staff meeting if I knew you were here."

My mother stood, brushing some nonexistent lint off her dress. It wasn't even lunchtime, but my mother looked like she was going to a cocktail party. Miriam Livingston didn't know the meaning of dressing down.

"No need. I was just passing through."

She held her arms open, and I grasped her gently, trying not to react to the heavy smell of mint on her breath. My stomach sank. I really hoped she hadn't been drinking this early. Normally I would pretend I didn't notice, but my mom just got out of rehab for the second time and we were really hoping it worked this time.

"Where were you before this? Did you have breakfast out?"

I thought I'd been so subtle, but my mother frowned. "Yes, I had breakfast out. With water. I just used mouthwash before I came here, that's all."

"Sorry, Mom. I just worry about you, that's all."

She shrugged that off and instead glanced behind us toward the door. "I'm worried about you with everything that's happened. But I guess I shouldn't now that you have your very own guard dog at the door. You know I like them young."

"Mom," I warned, hoping that for once Dylan wasn't paying attention.

He'd been giving me a lot of space all day and hadn't said a word about why he was here this morning instead of Oskar. Although I was sure Oskar hadn't told him the real reason he didn't want to be around me was because I'd thrown myself at him.

The memory of how things had gone down would haunt me until I was in the grave. In my defense, I'd been tired and feeling vulnerable. Or at least that was what I was telling myself.

It was the worst cliché, the rich girl falling for her body-guard because he was buff and available, and she didn't have time to date anyway.

Ugh, how embarrassing.

Did he think I was the type to throw myself at random men all the time? Considering how we'd met, me being drunk off my ass alone in Vegas, he must think I was completely irresponsible. Something about Oskar seemed to bring out my most impulsive qualities. It was like I lost my head looking at him and then did all the things I knew better than to do.

So in a way, it was really all his fault. Yeah, I liked the sound of that much better.

"You're just like your father. Always worried about what people think." Mom sat down in the chair in front of my desk, watching as I searched over the surface for my planner.

"Did you see a small planner when you came in? It's always on the right corner of my desk."

I tried not to let on how much it was bothering me that I couldn't find it. Even though everything was on my digital calendar, I liked the routine of writing things out in a paper planner. I'd been doing it since college, and it made me feel confident and in control to see all my goals and plans written out in my own handwriting.

When I looked up again, my mom was watching me with a slightly sad expression.

"I worry that I'll come see you one day and you'll be still glued to this desk with one foot in the grave. You have to let go and live sometimes because there's no reset button on life."

"Mom, are you okay?"

Before she could answer, my father appeared in the door-way. "Miriam, I didn't know you'd be here today."

There was a long moment of uncomfortable silence before my mom stood. My father walked over to her and placed a perfunctory kiss on her cheek while I tried not to watch.

It always made me sad to see my parents interact. They were cordial in the way you were to distant relatives you didn't like very much. But at least they were polite. There were rarely any dramatic arguments or fights in the Livingston household. No, my parents had simply agreed that they existed best apart from each other, and my father had moved into a different wing of the house. Very civilized.

And just as depressing.

Probably because a secret part of me worried that maybe I was just as cold and emotionless as they seemed to be. Was that my fate, to live alone in a separate part of the house from whomever I eventually married? Staying together not because we were in love but only because divorce was considered so unseemly?

"I wanted to ask your opinion on something, Hailey, but it can wait." My father looked like he was ready to run out of the room, but my mother beat him to it.

"No, don't leave. I have a spa appointment anyway. Just remember what I said, dear." She gave me a quick kiss on the cheek and left with an appreciative glance at Dylan.

My father tugged at his tie nervously. "What was your mother going on about?"

"Nothing. I think she just wanted to make sure I was okay after the attack."

I could tell he wanted to say something else, but in the end he decided not to. Which was entirely descriptive of our family dynamics, wasn't it? My mother did something reckless, and my father stuck his head in the sand while I kept working and Evan ignored us all.

At least avoidance was a family trait.

***

Oskar

Calling in sick was childish, yet I'd done it again today. Tyse had taken my first shift and Dylan had taken over from him. But in the end, I decided that avoidance was better than the alternative.

And... cue the way-too-detailed flashback. Fuck, my memory was too good as I remembered Hailey's lush little body squirming all over my lap. That moment, while clearly a bad idea, was going to fuel all of my shower jerkoff sessions for the next few years. The girl was hell on my control.

If I spent any time around Hailey right now, I wouldn't remember all the reasons we needed to be apart.

I was weak. There. I'd admitted it. An honest man could take a good, long, hard look at himself and face up to his mistakes and his weaknesses. And Hailey was my biggest weakness. She made me forget about all the bad shit I was running from and made me think about clouds and puppies and all that touchy-feely shit that men like me didn't deserve.

Two days apart was probably not enough to put a damper on whatever the hell this was between us. Any longer and Noah would wonder what the hell was wrong with me. I hardly ever got sick. None of us did. But it would have to be enough time for the memory of her swollen lips and sparkling eyes to fade.

It would have to be, since nothing could ever come of it.

Another text message came through from Dylan. He'd been sending me a stream of commentary all day about the people coming and going from Hailey's office. I think he was just trolling me at that point, since he'd seen me last night and knew I wasn't actually sick.

Dylan: You picked a hell of a day to skip out.

Oskar: Is everything okay?

Dylan: The mom just came by and as she went in whispered, "Aged wine is the best."

Doubling over, I ignored Matthias's annoyed look. Seriously, I needed to frame some of these messages just so I could blow them up and hang them around the office to torture Dylan with later. Not that there was anything wrong with a little cougar love. I didn't discriminate, and I'd learned some of my best sexual tricks from older women over the years. But the image of Hailey's conservative mother putting the moves on an incredibly uncomfortable Dylan was just comedy gold.

A few minutes later, a string of messages came in one after the other, making my phone sound like an angry bird chirping.

Dylan: Wow, I just overheard her telling Hailey that she "likes them young." Should I be worried?

Dylan: She just grabbed my ass.

Dylan: Dude, seriously this wasn't just a typical ass grab. Her fingers separated the cheeks!

Dylan: I've never felt so disrespected.

Dylan: Tell Noah that I want to file a complaint. This is an unsafe work environment.

Oskar: Will do.

Dylan: Wait, you know I was just kidding, right?

Dylan: Oskar?

Dylan: Oh, stop fucking with me!

I smothered my laugh with my hand. I decided not to answer. It was way more fun to leave him hanging and wondering if I'd actually told Noah anything.

"Are you even listening, mate?" Matthias's accent was more pronounced when he was annoyed.

"I am. Just thinking, that's all."

He knew I was lying, no doubt, but the tatted-up Englishman also wasn't the type to pry. He had plenty of secrets of his own, so he generally respected the rights of others to keep their business to themselves.

"Well, while you're thinking, do you mind moving your big arse off my desk?"

Technically, I was already supposed to have left by now, since I was due to meet with Hailey's father and also get some information while I was on the company premises. But it was way more fun to hang here when I knew my presence was annoying Matthias.

I grinned and planted another butt cheek on the furniture in question. For a former assassin, the guy was awfully fussy about his stuff, which made fucking with his head a game that never got old.

As long as I didn't touch any of the electronics in the room, it was all fun and games. But messing with one of his laptops was grounds for a fight.

Don't ask me how I knew that, either.

"Can you check into her family again?"

Matthias pretended he wasn't still looking at my ass parked on the edge of his desk. With a long-suffering sigh, I stood up. Since I was asking the guy for a favor, it was probably a good idea not to rile him too much. Not that he wouldn't grant the favor. Matthias took his work very seriously and would always go above and beyond for a client.

But he'd definitely find some subtle way to make me pay for pissing him off. On second thought, his methods probably wouldn't be that subtle. The dude did love knives, after all.

"I already finished background checks on the whole family. They're clean. Boring, but clean."

"Yeah, but I figure there might be something that pops out to you on a second look. Maybe there's a cousin who wants in on the family business. Hell, maybe the mom is tired of being sent to rehab and has decided to engage in a more domestic sort of chaos. It could be anything, but I'll feel better the more we know."

Matthias shrugged. "Did you get a bad feeling from the mom?"

"Haven't met her yet but according to Dylan, she's a real piece of work. Speaking of, I need to get going. I just want to wrap this one up. The sooner, the better."

The whole way over to Livingston Perfumes, I reviewed what we knew so far. Hailey was a workaholic and didn't have much life outside of her job, which increased the likelihood that her attack was related to Livingston Perfumes in some way. Her parents weren't divorced but should be, and her mother was way more aggressive than she appeared. Her brother seemed to be the classic case of a poor little rich boy with too much money and not enough actual work to do.

Basically, her case was like tons of other cases that we'd solved pretty quickly. So what were we missing about this one?

When I arrived at Livingston Perfumes, I sent a silent prayer that Hailey wouldn't be visiting her father at the exact moment that I was there. I was supposed to give him an update and also get some personnel files that Matthias had requested.

After parking, I used the special keycard I'd been issued to bypass the usual wait for the elevator and go directly to Hailey's floor. Before the doors closed, I saw Evan come out of an unmarked door in the garage and rush to a vehicle parked all the way at the edge of the lot. He looked over his shoulder before he got in the car and then immediately the vehicle started pulling out of the space.

Where was he going in such a rush? We had very little information about Hailey's brother other than he was two years older and worked directly with her father running the company. Or at least that was his listed job description. It didn't seem as though he actually did much work.

It was probably nothing, but I'd long ago learned to trust my instincts, so I sent a quick message to Matthias. If he was going to dig deeper into Hailey's family, it wouldn't hurt to start with her brother. There was definitely more going on there than what was on the surface.

I laughed softly to myself thinking about the text messages I'd received from Dylan earlier. There was definitely more to this family if Hailey's bodyguard wasn't even safe from a friendly grope at the hands of her mother. Normally I would have called Hailey after that and teased her about it, but that kind of stuff had to stop.

We weren't friends, and we couldn't be lovers. That was just the way it had to be.

Hailey

How long could he avoid me?

Well, so it seems, a while.

If he would just talk to me, we could figure out what was going on. My mind kept replaying his hands in my hair as he'd kissed me, his tongue sliding over mine, his hands on my hips as he dragged me under him, the sexy grind of it. It was a miracle I hadn't spontaneously combusted by now.

I needed help. Real help, because clearly, I had no idea what I was doing.

At this point, the man was completely avoiding me. I hadn't seen him in a day. No, that was not true. I briefly saw him yesterday morning when he legitimately ran away from me.

Tyse—I guessed he was new, as everyone called him the new kid—had been escorting me down to the car to drive me into work, and Oskar had come out of the gym. The moment he saw me, he'd frozen, and actually scooted around and run back into the gym. I'd seen him peeking out as the elevator door closed. A grown man, running away from *me*. If he didn't want me, fine. But at least he should be man enough to say so. Not kiss me like that and then just leave me.

Maybe there's a reason. Like the last time? I still wasn't sure how much I believed him about what had happened before. But I wanted to know. And now that he'd woken up the woman I'd buried deep inside, I went to bed every night frustrated, irritated, and so damn horny I was ready to start humping my pillow. And that was his fault.

I needed an expert.

Good thing I had one of those on speed dial. I flopped on the bed, my shoes dangling off the ends of my feet as I dialed Priya.

She answered on the second ring. "What's up, buttercup?"

God, I missed her. Ever since she'd gone to graduate school at UCLA, it had been hard to keep as close in touch as we used to be.

She was my best friend, and I spoke to her maybe twice a week. We used to talk that many times a day. But work and school was a real hindrance in our bestie goal situation. "How's school? Are you in the middle of something? Studying?"

"I know you're not wasting our two calls a week to ask me about classes. What gives?"

"Nothing. I'm curious about school."

"Come on, you didn't call to ask me about my dusty professors or that TA I'm banging."

"What?" I sat straight up.

"What?" Priya sputtered. "Never mind all that. What's wrong with you?"

I sighed. Where did I even start? "Um, okay. It's a long story, but—"

"This sounds like I need popcorn."

"You might. Hell, I need popcorn with extra butter."

Now I had a real craving. But I was going to ignore that. "Okay. You remember Vegas?"

"That epic trip where you got drunk for the first time, then got your cherry popped in royal fashion and discovered orgasms? Yeah, I remember that."

I flushed. This was the disadvantage of telling your best friend everything. "Well, that guy, he's back."

I could tell Priya dropped the phone because all I heard in the distance was, "What the fuck?"

She picked up the phone again. "Sorry. Dropped the phone. Okay, let me repeat. What the fuck?"

I laughed. "Yeah, exactly. The universe is conspiring against me."

"Or mother earth herself knows my girl could use a good oh, oh, oh... "

"Please stop."

"I'm not wrong. When was the last time someone took you to pound town?"

"Do you have to say it like that?"

"Look, I'm just getting you ready now, because when I come to visit in a couple of days, you'll get the full effect in person."

I was really looking forward to her trip here. Hello! I guess she'd have to stay here in the penthouse. I didn't really know how that was going to work. I would have to ask later.

"So, he works for a security firm here in New York. And when Dad decided I needed security—"

"Wait, why would your father think you need security?"

Yeah, so maybe I hadn't exactly told her about what was going on yet. "Remember the boutique thing from last week?"

"You mean the reason we haven't talked in two weeks? Yeah, I remember."

"Well, some idiot tried to grab me off the street."

"Oh my God. Way to bury the fucking lead."

"Priya, I'm fine."

"That does not sound fine. Did you sever his balls? Please tell me you severed his balls."

"No, I did not. But I did hit him really good in the nose. There was blood everywhere."

I could almost see Priya's satisfied nod. "Yeah, that's my girl."

"Don't be too proud of me. I basically forgot every single self-defense class I've ever taken in my life. I felt like one of those weak girls with flailing arms and screaming. Always screaming."

"Hey, you got away. That's all that matters."

"I suppose so. Anyway, it freaked Dad out. And he said I needed to have security."

"Yes, Papa Livingston. Protect our girl. And God, please tell me these security guys are hot!"

"How are we friends?"

"Because the goddess herself saw fit to bless you."

"Me and the goddess are going to have to have a chat. Anyway, so Dad insisted, and then I'm at the security firm, and out walks the hottest Viking specimen I have ever seen in my life. Sure enough, it's the guy from Vegas, and my whole body clenched because it went and remembered his touch."

"Tell me more." I could almost see Priya leaning forward toward the phone, trying to climb inside so she could get a better view of the story.

"There's nothing more to tell. I turned tail and ran."

"This story sucks."

"I just— I don't know. To see him again... and he acted like I should be happy to see him after the way he left me, and I just was so pissed I had to get out of there before I lost it."

"My God, I love when Little Miss Spitfire comes out to play. You are so controlled 90 percent of the time. Good to see you lose it just a little."

"When I lose it, bad things happen. Besides, I could tell it was what he wanted, for me to engage with him. So I didn't. Sure as hell, he was pissed."

"You know what? Maybe that's not a bad tactic because that would just make him want to pursue."

"Not exactly."

"What?"

I sighed. "Okay, so I didn't want the security. But they insisted. Dad insisted. And then the Viking was put on my detail."

"Yes, we're back in bodyguard territory. Please tell me he's a strong, silent type like Kevin Costner, and you are the fabulous diva type like Whitney Houston, and then there's bang. Much bang."

"No bang. Well, I just—I don't want a repeat."

"Yes, you do. If anyone could use some orgasms right now, it's you. You are wound so tight."

She was not wrong there.

"Orgasms do not fix everything."

"Yes, they do. Okay look, you need this guy. First, apparently, you need protecting, which we're going to discuss when I get there in ridiculous detail. But also, he's the only one who has unlocked the orgasm code with you. You need to take that stick out of your ass and replace it with something much more fun."

"Priya."

"What? I'm just saying, a little anal wouldn't hurt." She cracked a laugh. "See what I did there?"

I flushed and covered my face as if she could see me. "What did I do to deserve you?"

She cackled. "Fine, forget the anal. I'm just saying. Let his stick do the thawing. Wherever you may like it. I mean, you almost married a guy who was physically incapable of providing you orgasms. Can you imagine what hell that would have been?"

Ugh, I groaned. After Oskar had left me in Vegas, I dated Steven Elk. At the time, he was VP of Operations. He'd been transferred to our Paris offices since then. He was nice. And dependable. And very decent. Your basic nice guy.

He was a nice guy.

The problem was every time we were in bed, I had zero orgasms. Mr. Eight Seconds, as Priya had dubbed him, was not the most adept at making me come. He didn't liked to go down. And when we did have sex? *Eight seconds.* So the whole thing was just... God, miserable. And I'd been miserable because I couldn't even talk about what was upsetting me or how I was feeling in the situation, so I eventually broke off the engagement. And weirdly, he had seemed confused by it.

"God, please don't remind me."

"All I'm saying is this guy seems to know how to make your body hum. So get you some orgasms and work out whatever scenario you guys have going on. Then when this is all over, you'll be ready for someone new. You just need him to teach you the code, so you can teach someone else."

"Unfortunately, I think the code is him. God, I just look at him and my whole body is humming and zipping. The problem is now *he's* ignoring *me.*"

Anger seeped into her voice. "What do you mean, ignoring you?"

"I mean, more like avoiding me. We kissed the other night."

"Woohoo! Yes, girl. Get some."

"I wish. He kissed me and then stopped, and then he fed me some bullshit about how it was dangerous to be around him and he didn't want to do that to me, and basically he left me horny and pulsing and unable to think about anything else, except his stupid lips. And now, he's avoiding me. Straight-up avoidance."

"That is a man that wants you so bad he doesn't know what to do with himself."

"Are you sure about that? Because I get the impression that's not a real thing. When a guy wants you, he wants you."

"Mark my words, he wants you. He just has a funny way of showing it. Also, you are *hot*, girl. He would be lucky to be with you. So why don't you remind him of that? And if you don't know how, when I get there we will make him weep."

And that was why I missed her. "Thank you."

"Anytime bestie. Besides, you just remember who you are and that you don't need him. You just need the orgasms he can provide you. And we'll just have to find you someone else if he is uncooperative. If he doesn't realize how awesome you are and how lucky he is, then he doesn't deserve you. But if he's just running scared, you know how to make him bend to your will."

"Do I?"

"Yes. You just have to go after exactly what you want, just like you do at the company, and be unwilling to take no for an answer."

Okay, I could do this.

Liar. You have no idea how to do this.

"Um, how do I do this?"

Priya laughed. "Ever heard of naked under a trench coat? Pretty much works every time."

"You know what? A trench coat I've got. I can do this."

"Of course you can. Hailey Livingston with a plan is completely unbeatable."

"He's not going to know what hit him."

Oskar

Hailey was watching me.

She had been watching me all day. I smiled to myself. Even when we were trying not to be obvious, anyone could see the sparks flying between us. It had been pretty bad over the last couple of days. Every single slide of her gaze had my body rigid, tight.

The guys had noticed, for sure. And because she was living here, they'd been pretty good about it. But when we were out, God, Jonas couldn't shut the fuck up. And Rafe. I guess all those years of me giving him shit for, you know, his former job killing people, he was using the opportunity to just give it back to me.

That was fine though, as long as she wasn't uncomfortable. But for dinner, our honorary grandmother, Nonna, brought lasagna, so the whole gang was there. I mostly had held on to Izzy and volunteered to feed her because when you were holding a baby, you didn't have to talk to anyone. You were mostly trying to keep lasagna out of your hair and her hair. But then Rafe took his niece, which left me with no baby as a shield.

And yes, I knew how it looked using a baby as a shield. It was terrible.

Desperate times.

But after dinner, with everyone else off to bed, I needed to get away from Hailey. I didn't want to leave, but the looks she kept giving me... I was only a man. I was going to crack. So it was better I got the fuck away.

"I'm going to head to bed."

She glanced at the clock. "It's only ten."

"Is it?" How could it be so early? It felt like it had been six solid hours since the awkward dinner from hell began.

"And we're not finished with the movie." Hailey looked over at the paused movie still displayed on the TV.

She'd never seen *The Avengers*, so Matthias and I had insisted she needed a comic book instruction from the experts.

Matthias's fiancée, Gemma, was out on a job for ORUS, their secretive former employer. She wouldn't return until tomorrow. So Matthias was currently my wingman and my personal shield because the poor baby had gone to bed hours ago.

But then some data breach alarm for the Winston Isles account had gone off, and Matthias had to go deal with that, which left me and Hailey alone.

"I'm really tired. And not feeling so well. Maybe it was too much lasagna."

Internally I cringed. I needed to get away from her, but conjuring up images of food poisoning wasn't the ideal way I wanted to do that.

Hailey's brow wrinkled at that. "Oh, all right. I guess I'll finish the movie by myself."

I would not say that I ran. I did not run. I walked briskly out of the living room, down the hall, and then into the guest room I was using. *Holy shit.* I leaned back against the door, breathing deep and heavy.

My dick, unhelpful as ever, throbbed. And because I was an idiot and still wearing the sweatpants from my earlier workout, there was no way she wouldn't have noticed my dick trying to jump out at her.

I banged my head against the door once, trying to clear the fog. What the hell was wrong with me? She was just a woman.

Yeah, genius. She's got tits and an ass, and a face so breathtakingly beautiful you could cry. But I'd met lots of women. They were beautiful too. Why this one?

Because she matters. I knew what would happen if a guy like me was with a girl like her. She was way too innocent. And she would get hurt.

Frustrated, I dragged my T-shirt up over my head and tossed it somewhere in the vicinity of a hamper. I'd get it in the morning. I hadn't been kidding when I said the guest rooms weren't as well appointed as the rooms we actually used. The room was fine. Plush carpet, sparse decorations, but no pictures, no books, and the bed was smaller. That was the worst part.

I'd had a custom bed made for me. It was just the way I liked it. Big enough so my toes didn't hang off and wide enough I could stretch and roll around in it. This bed was a standard king. My limbs were falling off.

Quit complaining. Get to bed. Ignore it.

I left my sweats on and climbed into the bed, trying to force my brain to shut off.

Tomorrow, I'd have to deal with her all day. The way the rotation was currently scheduled, there was no way I could avoid her detail. Especially as I'd begged to be on her service. So I was going to need all the rest I could get.

After forty-five minutes of me tossing and turning, there was a quiet knock at the door and I sat up. "Come in."

The door opened slowly, and my eyes adjusted to the light peeking through. I saw it was Hailey.

"Are you okay?" I sat up.

"I um, I couldn't sleep. I had a bad dream," she said. I swallowed hard. *Oh shit.* I wasn't strong enough for this. "Can I sleep with you?"

Me? She wanted to fucking sleep with me? My dick was on team hell-fucking-yes. My brain was on team what-the-fuck.

Fuck. Say something. And don't let it be, *get the fuck into bed.* I cleared my throat. "Um, you know what? That's not the best idea. Come on. I'll take you back to your room."

Even in the shadows, I could see the pinch of her lips as her brow furrowed. That was not what she expected me to say.

I took the covers off and climbed out of the bed. The only problem with that was my dick was still hard. I knew my sweats hung low on my hips, and I was pretty sure I had a decent-sized dick print going on. Hailey's gaze scanned my chest. Then it dipped down lower. She chewed her bottom lip, and I groaned. "Come on. Let's get you back to your room."

With every step, my dick slapped against my leg as if to remind me that he was there and needed attention. Preferably from someone *other* than me. I took her to my room, opened the door, and let her in. "Get back in the bed, okay?"

She frowned at me. "Will you stay with me until I fall asleep?"

I swallowed hard. *Shit.* "Um, okay, just get in." I cleared my throat again. "Get into bed. I'll sit in the chair right here and keep you company until you fall asleep."

She chewed her bottom lip, and I knew that I was losing this battle. Why had I gotten out of that bed? And then, Hailey did the unexpected. She pulled on the knot of her robe, separated the panels, and dropped it.

"You can stay here, or you can go back to your room. And if you go back to your room, I'll just come back to you. I'm pretty sure you don't want me walking around like this."

I knew what I *should* do. I did. I really fucking did. But Hailey was naked. And *scheisse*. I wasn't that strong. "Fuck it," I said, and I reached for her.

CHAPTER THIRTEEN

Hailey

I'd wanted this, hadn't I? *So why are you suddenly so terrified?*

What if I wasn't as good as I thought I was? What if I felt different? *You're being stupid.*

Oskar tipped my chin up, and his gaze pierced mine. His pupils were so dilated I could barely see the ice blue of his irises, and I wondered what he was thinking. There was more than lust in that dark gaze of his.

"What's the matter, Hailey? What are you afraid of? Me?"

I shook my head. Oskar's voice lulled me into a trance,

while his soft touch seduced me, forcing me to forget my name, where I was, who I was with. My brain struggled for the right words. "I-I-I'm not afraid."

"You sure about this, Hailey? If I go here with you, there is no going back. Get used to me being inside you... a lot. Because I've been dying to get my hands on you. My hands are shaking."

His head dipped, and I held my breath. Ready for the electric shock that was Oskar to course through my body, igniting it from the inside. But his lips hovered just over mine. As if waiting for me to expose myself and bare all. I'd already bared my body, but he was waiting for my soul.

I swallowed hard. My shoulders rigid with tension, I forced myself to breathe. Deliberately, I rolled my shoulders, like the shedding of my protective shell was a physical barrier I had to unstrap, unbuckle, and unlace to step out of.

A little voice inside told me to let go, and for once, I listened. I didn't have to be strong. I didn't have to protect myself. I could simply be.

Meeting his gaze, I held it. I wouldn't back away; I couldn't run away. I could let myself be seduced. Let him take over. Let someone else be strong.

Suddenly, the breath I exhaled felt like freedom. It felt like bliss.

***

Oskar

"My brave little butterfly. You look scared now. You okay with this? We can stop at any time if you're not."

I wanted her so bad, just the hint of her perfume was enough to have me throbbing and running off to the shower for relief. But I didn't want her scared. I was doing everything in my power to make sure she wasn't scared. But fuck, I wanted her. I wanted her willing and ready and desperate. At least that would match how I'd been feeling since I'd seen her again.

Her gaze held mine. "Y-yeah." She licked her lips. "I'm okay."

When I pulled her to me, my hands shook a little. What the hell was wrong with me? I'd already slept with her once. But that was a long time ago, and we'd both changed since then. I'd have to learn what pleased her all over again. If I was going to cross the line, then I was going to do it irrevocably and with flourish. I wanted her hoarse from screaming my name. My inner caveman wanted her limp from so many orgasms she couldn't walk tomorrow. But that would take thorough exploration... Good thing I was up for the task.

I spanned her waist with my hands, dragging her flush against me. She gasped, and her gaze snapped to mine. The thundering of my heartbeat was all I could hear as I focused on her parted lips.

Last time we'd done this I'd had... some control issues. I'd gone way too fast. I'd been so desperate to get inside her, I hadn't gone slowly enough. I didn't know she was a virgin then. I should have guessed. I'd been way too rough with my hands, my mouth, my dick.

I'd left faint bruises on her hips from my grip. There'd been hickeys all over her tits, and she'd been sore after the first time. I'd tried to go easier the second time, but she'd been busy chasing another orgasm and had gripped me *just so* as she came, and I'd given her another too-rough session, with my teeth on her neck as her pussy convulsed around the length of my dick. My plan had been to slow things way down the next time, but I'd never gotten to fulfill that promise.

Go slow, you idiot.

I could do this. Give her what I'd meant to give her then.

I dipped my head, brushing my lips against hers softly. Immediately, she sighed into my mouth and wound her hands into the hair at the nape of my neck. Like liquid napalm, fire flashed quick, and I groaned.

I slid my tongue over hers, my hands sliding over her bare ass, bringing her tight up against me. Fuck, this was so good. Too good. *So much for slow, asshole.*

I tried to slow it down, take my time, but then she sucked my tongue into her hot, wet mouth, and I forgot for a moment that I was supposed to be taking things slow. Focusing on drawing this out. I only wanted to keep tasting her.

While she tried to wrestle control of the kiss from me, my hands fisted in the material of her robe, and I tugged up. Her sudden, shocked intake of breath was all I needed to take charge again. I lifted her up until she wrapped her legs around me, but I didn't deposit her on the bed. Instead, I turned to the door and braced her against it. My lips on hers, I muttered, "*Fuck,* Hailey. I don't have enough control with you."

"Is that bad?"

She used my shoulders as leverage and arched her body so that her slick heat met the bulge in my sweats. My dick had probably worn a hole in the damn things. I'd probably stop traffic if I went out like this. "Fuuuuck me."

"That is the point, right? If you're just teasing me, I might actually kill you."

She worked her hips in a figure eight, and my eyes crossed. My shy little butterfly knew how to move her body. Who'd been teaching her? Fuck. I shoved that thought out of my head. "Hailey." Her name was more grunt than English.

Hell, I couldn't even be sure it *was* English. All kinds of dirty images and ideas were floating through my mind at the moment. Slipping into German was just as likely. I knew how to say dirty things in French too. I could manage in Italian if I concentrated. Whatever I had to do to get her to let me show her.

Lust chased desire along my nerve endings. I had to find a way to gain control again. *You don't get to rush this time. Slow the fuck down.*

I reluctantly removed her hands from the nape of my neck and lifted them above her head as I encircled them. I licked at her lips very deliberately, before sliding my cock against her other satin-smooth lips.

She hissed, and her body shook. "Oskar. Please. I need you inside me. I feel like I'm going to explode if you don't make love to me."

Yeah, I knew the feeling. "Look at me, Hailey."

Her lids fluttered open, and her eyes were nearly black, her pupils were so dilated. As I kissed her again, my body rocked against hers, and she met every movement of my hips with her own. "You want me to take you like this? Hard and fast and up against the wall?"

She nodded. "I don't care how you take me. I just—" Her voice shook. "I have wished for this moment for years. Please just fuck me."

Hell yes. "Nope. You had it right the first time. I'm going to make love to you." I nuzzled her neck as I slipped my hand up over her belly and palmed her breast. When my palm closed over her fullness, she whimpered, and I moaned. Her breasts were so full and firm. So soft and responsive.

"Oskar, please."

I kissed her again, savoring every flavor on her tongue,

sucking on it until she rocked into me in a steady rhythm. She fought my grip on her wrists, but I held firm. I wanted her to have a good, strong orgasm before I lost total control.

Slowly, I backed away from the kiss. Releasing her hands, I steadied her by the waist and set her back on the floor. Her eyes went wide with questions, but she didn't say anything. Merely followed my silent command as I turned her around.

"Oskar, what are you doing?"

"I'm taking care of you, butterfly. Like I should have our first time." I skimmed my hands up her torso, palming the soft globes and gently massaging. Her legs started to quiver when the massage turned from relief to sensual tease. Gently, I plucked the pebbled tips, and she dropped her forehead against the door.

"You'll have to forgive me, but I've had a mild obsession with your breasts since I first saw you in that bar. I have spent countless hours thinking about if they tasted the same, felt the same. Wondering if they were still as sensitive as I remembered. If you'd still like it if I used my teeth when I sucked on you."

Her breath came out ragged and sharp. "Oskar. I can't. You're killing me."

I plucked the tight buds again. "If you want me to stop, all you have to do is say so."

I trailed open-mouth kisses across her shoulders and the back of her neck as I played.

When she started to rotate her hips back against me, I swore and gritted my teeth at the red haze of lust clouding my vision.

"Lean forward for me."

She hesitated for a moment, but then did as I asked. I released her arms, then slid down her body. I rewarded her with a soft kiss on her slick lips, and she shivered. As I kneeled, I lapped at her cleft with long strokes. With my hands on her firm ass, I massaged then teased her by sliding a finger inside her slick channel.

Hailey cursed softly, but I continued my licking and stroking. Working my tongue over her clitoris while I penetrated her with my fingers. The slick walls of her core milked at my fingers, and I felt them quiver. Kissing her inner thighs, I encouraged her. "Come on, Hailey. Give me what I want." I continued to lick and stroke her until her whole body shook. *That's it. Come on.*

Finally, with a whisper of my name in the moonlight, she let go.

Hailey

I shook as Oskar picked me up and laid me on the bed.

Holy hell. That was even more intense than I remembered. All this time, I'd been convinced that I'd imagined how good it was. That I'd somehow amplified it. But no. I hadn't. If anything, I'd done the guy a disservice. Aftershocks rolled through my body, leaving me languid and foggy.

What was he doing to me? If I wasn't careful, I was going to get addicted. Then where would I be when he left again? I didn't know what we were doing, but that was one thing I was sure of. Oskar was spontaneous and fun. And outrageous. Guys like that didn't stick. After all, he'd left before. He'd explained, sort of, but presumably nothing had changed. I just needed to prepare for that eventuality.

He hooked his thumbs in his sweats then casually shucked

them like he hadn't been hiding some kind of tree trunk in there.

My eyes went wide, and I stared. *There is no way.*

You've slept with him before. It fits.

No. I must have imagined sleeping with him, because there was no way I stretched that much. A nervous laugh trilled out as I let my eyes drift closed.

His voice was soft but authoritative. "Hailey, look at me."

I shook my head.

His touch was soft on my cheek. "Shh, look at me."

I peeled my lids open. "Oskar, I—"

"I'm not going anywhere. I'm right here with you. All you have to do is touch me. Don't be nervous. All I'm here to do is make you feel good." He slid into bed beside me, and I had to scoot over to make room for him. "You with me?" he asked as he drew me close.

I swallowed hard and nodded against his chest as I inhaled. Sandalwood. I sighed and immediately relaxed. I loved that smell. The moment I was wrapped in his arms, I felt like I was exactly where I belonged.

Oskar pressed featherlight kisses along my temple, my forehead, my jawline, the tip of my nose. When he reached my lips, he barely skimmed them with his own, and I whimpered as heat spread through me. He angled his head and deepened the kiss, anchoring my face in his hands as he devoured me.

Desire spiked again as his expert tongue licked at the roof of my mouth. How in the world could he make me feel like this again?

As I met his tongue with mine, a spike of heat had me writhing against him. The crisp curls on his chest brushed my nipples, turning them into hardened peaks. His muffled moan made his chest rumble. And the friction against the sensitive peaks of my breasts sent a pull of desire straight to my core.

The length of his erection pressed into my thigh insistently, and I reached down to wrap my hand around the rigid length of it. A flare of panic seized me again when I realized my fingers didn't touch.

He muttered something in German that I could only assume was a swear, and his hips pushed into my hand insistently. "Jesus. Hailey—"

I could do this. I was terrified of making love to the tree

trunk, but I could make him feel good. With sure fingers, I continued stroking him, running my hands over the velvet-soft length of him. When I ran my palm over the sensitive tip, his hips jerked, and a drop of moisture leaked from the tip to lubricate my palm.

"Hailey. Fuck." My name came on a harsh breath, making me feel bold enough to repeat the action. His hand closed over mine as he directed my motions, and lust chased away the doubt. "God, woman." He stilled my hand and squeezed his eyes shut. "I have been dreaming about having you again." He ground his teeth as his hips jerked again and his dick twitched in my suspended hand.

I smiled against his lips. "When I saw you again, I wanted to hit you. Then I wanted to run my hands all over you."

He sucked in a strangled breath. "I would have been fine with both because it would have meant you touching me." He growled low and kissed me deep.

Just like that, any lingering doubt dissipated. His fingers dipped between my thighs, and I held my breath. God yes. He slipped a finger inside me, my body more than ready. Gently, his thumb caressed my clit and I moaned, parting my thighs to allow him better access.

"God, you are so wet. So ready." He pressed deeper, his fingers finding my G-spot and rubbing.

"Oh God, Oskar."

"Mmm?" he asked as he trailed kisses along my throat then my collarbone, eventually sliding to my breast. With his mouth poised over a nipple, he paused. His breath tickled my skin, and I writhed. "Say please."

I would slap him... later. But right then, I was down for doing what I had to in order to get his mouth on me. "Oskar, please."

"Please what?" His warm breath was a tease.

"Please kiss me."

He placed a kiss right above my breast. "Right there?"

I arched my back in frustration. "No, damn it. On my breast."

Oskar kissed the underside of my breast. "Oh, you mean here?"

"Oskar!" I threaded my hands through his hair. "Stop teasing me."

He kissed the underside of my other breast. "I like teasing

you." He hovered over the tip of my breast again. "You like it when I tease you." All the while his thumb continued to circle my clit. While I panted, he slid another finger into me, then a third.

He kept the pace nice and easy, no matter how much I angled my hips, moving against his fingers. Finally, he brushed his lips over my nipple, and I cried out.

With a deep chuckle, he settled his lips around my nipple, and a pull of lust pierced my core. Blood rushed in my head, and all I could think about was Oskar. His lips, his fingers. Like everything else in the world had vanished and all that mattered now was this moment, this time with him. Another orgasm danced on the edge of my senses, but I couldn't grasp it.

"Oskar, please. I need you to—"

"Shhh, I hear you." He removed his fingers from my heated skin and rolled his big body over mine, bracing himself over me. His erection nudged my cleft, and he swore. "You're so wet."

At that point, the need had chased away any fear. All I cared about was grasping that elusive orgasm, and I didn't care how I got there. I rotated my hips, sliding my cleft along the length of him. "Please, I need it..."

He dropped his forehead to mine and kissed me softly. When he rolled away from me, I whimpered. What the hell?

But I cut off my protest when he opened the bedside table and pulled out a pack of condoms. Magnums, of course.

He had himself sheathed in record time, and then he re-settled between my thighs. His tongue licked at my bottom lip before he nipped. "Now that you're here again, I'm not letting you go."

His erection slid against my slit before partially sliding into me. We both gasped. I met his gaze as he pierced my soul. In that moment I knew I would never be the same. His lips tight and brow furrowed, he kept eye contact as he retreated then slid forward again.

I held my breath as I clutched on to his shoulders. When he realized that I wasn't breathing, he reached between us, his thumb sliding over my clit with firm pressure.

That immediately had me exhaling a puff of breath, and my body relaxed. With another retreat and slide forward, he was fully seated inside me. And it felt—Holy shit. That last slide rubbed right over my G-spot, and I had to gasp.

With a cocky smirk, he retreated again, then slid home

again. Oh, that felt... full, yes, but also...wow. So delicious. So good. So. Damn. Good. "Oh God."

He removed his thumb from my clit and buried his hand in my hair. "I promised to take it slow this time. But God, you feel so good."

"This feels..." I couldn't even finish. The electric currents running through my body were making me dumb.

"I know." He kissed me again, his tongue mimicking what the thick length of him was doing. As he increased his pace, I dug my hands into his back. How the hell had I been scared?

I met him thrust for thrust. He kept his gaze on mine, never breaking the intimate connection as another orgasm coursed through me. *Oh God.* I bucked as the pleasure rolled through my body.

With rough, muttered words in German, Oskar dug his hands in to my hair, dropped his forehead to mine, squeezed his eyes shut, and held on tight as his orgasm pounded through his veins.

Before he collapsed, he whispered, "Too late to run now."

CHAPTER FOURTEEN

Oskar

"Let's get this meeting going." Noah glared at each of us around the table in turn, his way of reminding us to pay attention.

Okay, maybe he just glared at me. I couldn't help it that I had a bad habit of falling asleep during these things. Keeping a crew as diverse as ours in line was probably a full-time job so I couldn't fault the dude for trying to regulate. But there were times you just had to accept that certain things weren't going to happen.

Me staying awake during a status meeting was one of those things.

These meetings were important, but oftentimes they were an opportunity for Matthias to show off his research skills. Meaning, exciting for him and boring as hell for the rest of us. So I usually took it as an opportunity to catch up on some quality time with the backs of my eyelids.

"Okay, let's get started with the Livingston case. Where are we?" Noah leaned back in his chair, his fingers steepled.

And that was my cue to fall asleep. I'd gone over all the background info on the Livingston case a million times, but I couldn't turn my mind off. All I could see when I closed my eyes was Hailey dropping that robe. I rubbed a hand over my face and glanced around before pulling at the suddenly tight crotch of my jeans. Jesus Christ, the girl was trying to kill me.

That little maneuver was going down in history as one of the sexiest things I'd ever seen. Probably only topped by the weekend I'd first met Hailey. It was still as vivid in my imagination as the day it happened. She'd been a force to be reckoned with even then. Twenty-one years old, devastated but not broken, she'd captivated me with one look. Sure, it wasn't the smartest thing to get drunk with a stranger and cavort through Sin City, but damn if it hadn't been one of the best times of my life.

It was taking all of my will not to push the issue, but also there was a part of me that was just pathetically grateful she didn't want to call me out for my dumbass behavior that weekend. I sighed. In the moment, leaving had seemed like the best option. The only option. But with the advantage of time and a little maturity, I could see how my impetuous decision had cost us both. Because Hailey had been on her own all this time with no one to look out for her. It was the reason why we were here now discussing her case. Yes, my past was a shitstorm. And yes, there was a chance being with me could have put her in danger, but apparently she'd found danger on her own anyway. At least if I'd been around, I could have protected her before some asshole tried to abduct her from that alley.

If you'd still been together, that is.

There was no denying that my track record with relationships wasn't great. But that was because I'd never clicked with anyone the way I had with Hailey. I'd never wanted to stick around for longer than one night or a fun weekend. The only reason I'd managed to leave her the first time was because I did it before we had time to get completely attached. But something told me that if I hadn't bailed in the heat of the moment, I would have still been in Hailey's life.

Mainly because I couldn't imagine having the strength to leave her alone after we'd been together for a while. I already suspected there was no way I'd be able to just walk away after this assignment ended. After following her around, sleeping in her apartment, and now having her in my bed, there was no way. She was going to have to adjust to having a six-foot-plus shadow for the rest of her life.

"… is married."

The words permeated my brain, snapping me out of the near stupor I'd fallen into.

"Sorry, what did I miss?"

Matthias pointed at the screen. "Only the most important part. During the background check, I discovered that Hailey Livingston is married."

"What the actual fuck?" I stood so suddenly that my chair toppled over, making a loud sound on the polished concrete floor. A rage unlike anything I'd ever felt swept through me, and I had to bury my hands in my hair to keep from grabbing the closest person to me and throwing them through the wall.

"How the fuck did you miss that the first time around?"

Matthias moved closer, and then suddenly everyone was

standing. This was a firm filled with aggressive, testosterone monsters, and throwing down a verbal challenge like that was a great way to invite an afternoon of bloodshed. I fought dirty, but Matthias was dirtier and more skilled. Even I knew that, but at the moment, I just didn't give a shit.

Because in my head, I needed someone else to blame. I wasn't ready to accept my own part in this, and it was easier to point at someone, anyone, else.

"Okay, cut the shit. Both of you sit your asses down." Noah wasted no time getting between us, throwing off waves of aggression of his own.

"Matthias, finish the presentation. Oskar, sit your ass down or I'll put you down."

I picked up my chair and righted it. After another pointed look from Noah, I parked it and kept my mouth shut. I had to battle the insane jealousy that arose at the thought of Hailey having a husband. After our magical weekend together, it had been the most difficult thing in the world to leave Hailey behind. But I'd done it knowing it was best for her. I wanted more for her than a life in danger. I wanted her to have it all: a career, to fall in love, to have the family she'd always dreamed of.

It shouldn't be a shock to me that she'd pursued those things after I left. It was her right and with a woman as beautiful and sweet as Hailey, almost inevitable.

But after what we'd shared last night, I'd started to believe in the impossible. That maybe we could find a way around the things that had once kept us apart. Maybe I was just fooling myself, but it had been amazing to pretend that she was mine again. I wasn't ready to give that up.

"Okay, I'm cool now. Sorry, M."

Matthias actually grinned. "No problem. But if you're already off the rails now, wait until you learn more about her husband."

"Who is he? Is he involved? Does Hailey know that he's back?"

I shot out question after question, trying to quell the mounting panic that there was something out there we couldn't protect her from. Clearly Hailey didn't think her husband—my teeth ground at the thought—was any threat or she would have at least mentioned the guy.

Maybe that was the part that was bothering me the most. Hailey had never said anything about having a husband. After everything we'd still been avoiding each other. And I was furious about the news. Not exactly rational. But whatever.

"I built a profile about this guy. Wait until you see this." Still grinning, Matthias clicked a few more buttons, and then a huge image appeared on the screen.

An image of my face.

There was a pause as everyone at the conference table looked at each other, and then Ryan started laughing. Noah squinted at the image before sitting back in his seat. He didn't look any more amused than I felt.

Jonas leaned forward. "Is this a joke?"

Matthias shook his head. "Nah, mate. There's no joke. Hailey met her husband, Oskar, three years ago in Las Vegas. This guy is a real wanker. Look, I found more pictures of him."

He clicked another button, and a huge image of a naked ass appeared on the screen. There was a yellow butterfly tattooed on one cheek. It was an image I was very acquainted with since I saw it every morning when I got out of the shower. It served as my daily reminder to wonder what the hell I'd been thinking all those years ago.

When Noah's eyes flipped my way, I instantly shrank

down into my seat. "Where did you get that? Please tell me that's not floating around out there somewhere on the internet?"

"Oh no, don't worry. I took that one straight from your personal laptop." Matthias raised his eyebrows. It was clear from the rare smile on his face and maniacal glee in his eyes that he was enjoying this. A lot.

I groaned and covered my eyes with my hands. "Fucking hell. Is everything a joke to you? This is serious. Hailey is in danger and we don't have time for practical jokes."

Matthias leaned over the table, his face as serious as I'd ever seen it. "There is a marriage license registered in Nevada with your name and Hailey's name on it. This is not a joke. This is not a drill. What this is, is a major fucking problem."

Noah stood. "Everyone back to work. Matthias and Oskar, in my office. Now."

Hailey

I was completely absorbed in my work when I felt it. You know, that prickly feeling you got when someone was watching you. I always got the urge to swat at an imaginary spider because it felt like my skin was crawling.

Oskar stood just inside the doorway, leaning on the frame, watching me. The blue of his eyes looked even more intense for some reason. Maybe it was the light.

Or maybe it was because you missed him?

I tried to control the silly little smile that wanted to break free at the sight of him. Keep it cool. Keep it casual. I'd promised myself that I would not turn into a giggling, fluttery girl at the sight of him. Just because we'd slept together and just because he knew how to do some truly amazing things with his tongue was no reason to lose every bit of my self-respect.

But no, my inner girly girl was currently twirling her hair around her finger and blowing kisses. That little hussy had no shame.

My neck protested when I sat back and rolled my shoulders. "Oh hello."

There. That was perfectly casual and noncommittal. I thought it hit just the right balance between surprise and nonchalance.

"Are you ready to go?" He glanced around the office as if verifying that I was alone.

That's when I noticed how dark it was outside and how quiet it was. How long had I been buried in research? The clock in the upper corner of my computer boasted that it was after eight o'clock. I hadn't gone home that late all week. Having personal security had actually helped my work/life balance. It was a lot harder to justify staying late when someone else was waiting around for me.

"Yes, I am. I didn't realize it was so late. Sorry if I held you up."

"It's fine."

Something about him was really off today. Maybe he was feeling the awkwardness just as much as I was. We'd had sex and it had been amazing. The thought brought a private smile to my face. It was the understatement of the year to call sex with Oskar amazing. Blazing hot or ridiculously explosive would be more accurate. When I'd woken up this morning I had been sore in places that I didn't even realize I'd used the night before. The man was not only completely insatiable but had no limits. There was no filter on that dirty mouth of his, and he had no problem doing anything and everything that would bring me pleasure.

I wasn't sure if I was supposed to pretend like it was no big deal or send him a fruit basket for rocking my world. But it undoubtedly made things strange now that we were back in the real world.

Did I kiss him hello now?

Were we going to sleep in the same bed every night?

More importantly, would it happen again?

The whole ride back to the penthouse, Oskar barely said a word. I couldn't help but take a little mental ride back to the last time I saw him this quiet. To be fair, he was drunk and so was I. Vegas had a way of causing people to either go crazy or get very introspective and confess their deepest thoughts. Sometimes simultaneously.

But I didn't have the right to ask him what was going on in his head. Not yet. Just because we'd slept together, it didn't make us a couple. Especially since he hadn't said anything about the prior night.

Oh God.

Maybe this was his way of indicating that he didn't want to do it again. He'd rocked my world but that didn't mean the feeling was mutual. The sex might have been boring for him, and now he was working out a way to let me down easy. This was a pity silence.

No. I squashed all the self-defeating thoughts and forced myself to remember who I was dealing with. Oskar wasn't the type to tiptoe around his feelings. If he hadn't been into it last night, he would have just said so. And I might not have a lot of experience, but even I knew that having multiple orgasms, for both partners, was an indication that a good time was had by all.

But something was definitely wrong with him. I snuck another look at him. His profile gave nothing away. He was completely focused on the road.

After another five minutes, I finally couldn't take it anymore.

"Did something happen today?"

He laughed, but it was a bitter sound. "A lot of things happened today. You're going to have to be more specific."

"Is this about last night?"

I held my breath waiting for his answer. It would stink if

he didn't want a repeat, but at least it was better to know than to get the cold shoulder.

"No, it's not about last night. But we probably should talk about that. Later. We should talk about that later." He made a face but then clamped his lips closed again.

My heart sank. Okay, maybe my earlier assumption that Oskar would just tell me if he wasn't happy wasn't true. Because there was obviously something about last night that he was keeping from me. And it didn't seem like a positive memory.

"Well, I know it's none of my business but the last time you were this quiet, you were trying to figure out how to tell me we got tattoos while we were drunk."

He froze, and something about the expression on his face made me very nervous. "Funny you should mention that. How much do you remember about Vegas?"

I looked out the window, letting my eyes roam over the other cars and the pedestrians as we passed by. New York City at night used to be one of my favorite things but ever since the attack, it had lost some of its magic. Now I preferred to view the city from a bit of a distance. The windows in my apartment were perfect.

If I ever got to see them again, that is.

"I remember everything about Vegas."

"Not everything," he muttered.

Now that made me angry. If he didn't want to be close to me anymore, that was fine. I got it and the rational part of my brain agreed. Considering our history and how easily we both lost control when around each other, I could respect his wish to keep some distance. But he wasn't going to invalidate my memories and my experiences.

Vegas was a bad memory for me, only because it had started with such promise just to have it all crash and burn at the end. Those three days made up the most maddening, exhilarating, tender, and heartbreaking time of my life.

It had been three years, and every moment was so vivid it felt like it had happened just a few months ago instead of years.

If I was honest with myself, those times would probably be the most exciting I would ever have. How depressing was that?

"Listen, you may not want to be friends with me. Or lovers. Or anything. But don't make the mistake of thinking that you have me figured out. I remember Vegas like it was just this past weekend. Getting ditched by the man you're pretty sure you're falling in love with tends to leave a lasting impression."

The words hung in the air between us, and my breathing increased as I realized what I'd just said. Oskar looked over at me for as long as he could before his attention was pulled back to the road.

"You were in love with me."

"That's not what I said," I insisted. Even though it kind of sort of was exactly what I'd said.

We arrived back at Blake Security a few minutes later, and Oskar pulled into the same parking spot he always used in the back. I didn't wait for him before pushing open my door and getting out. I was humiliated enough that I'd just shouted that I was in love with him, but I definitely didn't need the uncomfortable song and dance that was sure to come as he figured out how to tell me that he'd never felt the same.

"Hailey—"

"We don't need to talk about it. Let's just go."

"Before we go upstairs, there's something you need to know. While we were in Vegas we did a lot of things."

Embarrassed and tired, I crossed my arms impatiently. "I know. We got really drunk. We had a lot of sex. My idea. And we got the worst tattoos ever. Pretty sure those were your idea."

"I deny that," Oskar drawled. "But what's undeniable is that we did other things that neither of us remembers. One of those things was get married."

CHAPTER FIFTEEN

Oskar

She was in shock. She had to be. Or at least that was what I assumed since Hailey hadn't said a word to me since I'd dropped the matrimonial truth bomb.

I followed her as we walked from the parking lot into the elevator and finally into the penthouse. Someone must have been looking out for me because for once, no one was there when we got home. Or if they were, they were in their rooms.

Seeing Matthias right then would have been a bad fucking road. Not that it was his fault. Logically I knew it wasn't.

But I wasn't in the mood to see that smug face right then. Not when Hailey looked like she'd just been coldcocked with a two-by-four.

"Say something. Please." I closed the door behind us once we were in my room.

Hailey dropped her bag by the door, for once not bothering to put it carefully away. Her shoes came off next, abandoned in the middle of the floor. She sat on the edge of the bed, her eyes far away.

"I don't know what to say. We're married." She whispered the last part, sounding horrified.

I would take offense to that if I didn't understand her position completely. Being the other half of this surprise marriage equation, I got the horror. Most of us felt as though we at least knew who we were and what our lives were about. Finding out something this important years after the fact just felt wrong. Like a betrayal except we had no one to blame.

Well, I was going to blame this one on Vegas. That city had a way of fucking with you even years after you'd left.

"I know this is a shock. Matthias just told me today. Well,

he told the whole damn team. Seemed pretty happy to fuck with my head."

Hailey's eyes latched onto mine. "So you had no idea about this?"

"Of course not. You think I wouldn't have said anything? Like, 'oh, hi Hailey. Nice to see you again, *wifey*'?"

She cringed. "Good point. That was a dumb question, but I'm trying to work out in my head how we could be married but have no idea. I remember that weekend."

"So do I. But I have to admit I mainly remember us being naked for a really long time. I wasn't particularly inclined to care about what happened before we got to that point."

We shared a brief, private smile. Yeah, my memories of that sex-fueled weekend were pretty stellar. Nothing could top losing all your inhibitions with someone you were crazy compatible with. I coughed, trying to think of anything other than Hailey naked.

Not the time, dude. She was finally talking to me again, and the glassy look had cleared from her eyes. I didn't think a big eyeful of my hard dick was going to be the best way to keep this conversation going.

Suddenly Hailey gasped. "Oh my God. That was our

honeymoon. That's why there were so many champagne bottles everywhere when we woke up. We were celebrating."

I thought back to the aftermath of that weekend. She was right. There had been a crazy number of bottles strewn around the room on Sunday afternoon, but I'd just assumed we'd kept ordering it because it was Hailey's favorite or something.

It hadn't seemed that odd that Drunk Oskar would want to order his lady's favorite drink. But apparently Drunk Oskar was actually ordering his *wife* more champagne to celebrate their *honeymoon*.

Drunk Oskar was a romantic. Surprise, surprise.

"I know this is a shock. But really, it's not that big of a deal. We can fix it."

Hailey's eyes swung to me, as sharp as daggers. "Not that big of a deal? Oskar, we're married. Joined in holy matrimony. Everything about that is a big deal. And you saying that just proves how little we know about each other."

Hailey

The next morning was awkward.

Looking at Oskar brought up way too many unresolved feelings, none of which I was ready to examine or deal with yet. And I suspected that he felt the same since he seemed more than happy to leave when Ryan showed up at lunchtime to relieve him.

I sighed. He hadn't offered much more than some vague excuse as to why he was leaving early, and I didn't ask. Although he had promised to be back in time to pick me up since I was working late tonight before picking up my best friend from the airport.

Despite everything I smiled. Priya's visit couldn't have come at a better time. Not only did I need a distraction from Oskar and all this craziness, but she would be able to help me figure out what to do next. My best friend's usual brand of no-bullshit advice was exactly what I needed right then.

A quick glance at the time in the upper corner of my computer screen told me that it was already past six o'clock. The final proofs I was waiting on from the art department should be along any time now.

Normally I would have been annoyed to be stuck at the

office waiting on something that was actually due a few days ago but that night, I was glad for the distraction.

It was better than going back to the Blake Security penthouse and having to put on a smiling face for everyone else. Or having to try to avoid Oskar when we were living in the same place.

"Hailey! You're still here."

I looked up to see my dad standing in the doorway holding a small cardboard box. When he noticed where I was looking, he held it up.

"Just dropping off some samples the R&D team wanted you to evaluate. I didn't think you'd actually be here though. You've been leaving earlier the past week."

Something about that made my back stiffen. I stayed late all the time, so it felt odd that he was only noticing the days when I left at a decent hour.

"I left earlier since that was easier for my security. You know, the security you insisted that I have."

He nodded. "I'm glad things are working out. I feel much better knowing you're protected. So why are you here so late tonight? Is everything confirmed for the launch party?"

"Everything is on track. You don't need to worry."

"Have you confirmed with the event venue that they'll have adequate security?"

I nodded. "Yes, they provide security, and I've also arranged for our own as well."

He looked around and rocked back on his heels. "Good. Good. I'm sure things will be perfect. So why are you still here? You should go home and relax. Or go out with your friends and have some fun."

I stared at him in confusion. What alien had taken over my father's body? Because there was no other explanation for why he'd encourage me to go out and be frivolous instead of working on things that mattered.

"The art department will be delivering the final art any moment now. That's what I'm waiting on."

"What? The launch is only a week away!"

I put up my hands. "We're well aware. They were just making a few minor adjustments that I asked for."

He sighed. "I'm worried about you, Hailey. You've always been a perfectionist, but this launch seems to have taken over your life."

Even though I knew his words were coming from a genuine place, something about it enraged me. Wasn't this what he'd taught me? All my life, I'd looked up to my father and wanted to be just like him. Well, mission accomplished. I was a chip off the old block. I worked hard every night and then went home to work some more. I'd given everything to this company, and now he was telling me that was wrong?

"You're calling me a workaholic? I guess I got it honestly then since you're the same way."

My father looked up sharply at my pointed words. "Excuse me, young lady?"

I could feel the emotion rising and saw myself as if I was floating above us. How had I gotten to this point? Yelling at my father, being short with my staff. But I knew that it was my anger at Oskar taking over my life. He wasn't here for me to yell at, so I was taking it out on everyone else.

Which wasn't right. It wasn't me.

It was rare for us to argue, but even rarer for me to speak to him like that. I was raised to respect my elders and to think before I spoke. Usually I could handle anything, but it was clear that I'd lost all my composure.

And I knew exactly who to blame for it.

It was time for me to leave before we said things we couldn't take back.

"I'm sorry, Dad. I appreciate what you're saying. Really, I do. But I'm doing what I've been taught my whole life to do. This is what I'm good at, and I'm proud of what I've accomplished here."

He ran his hands over his face. For the first time in a long time, I looked at my dad and saw him without the rose colored glasses of a young child who worshipped her father. He looked tired. And older.

And maybe a little defeated.

"I know that, baby. I didn't mean to imply otherwise. You have to know how proud I am of you."

"I do. Thanks. I'm just working so hard on this launch because I want it to be special for Mom."

A small smile tugged at his lips. "This is going to be our biggest launch yet. I can already tell."

He walked out, but the low set of his shoulders proved that our argument had affected him as much as it did me. I hated to fight with anyone but least of all with the man I'd always admired most. I flopped back into my seat and threw the pen I was holding down. The clattering sound it made was mildly satisfying but not nearly enough to match the turmoil inside.

I would probably need a battering ram for that.

"Trouble in paradise, hmm?"

I looked up to see Evan leaning against the doorframe with a satisfied smirk on his face.

"Just a disagreement. It happens."

He shrugged. "Never thought I'd see the day Miss Perfect didn't immediately get her way. Must be hard having to come down to reality with the rest of us, huh?"

After the emotional showdown with my father, I was in no mood to deal with Evan's crap. "Why do you hate me so much? You realize it's not normal to enjoy seeing your own sibling having a hard time?"

He straightened his tie but wouldn't meet my eyes. "I don't hate you. It's just hard to live in your perfect shadow sometimes."

"I'm not perfect and I've never pretended to be. I wish we could be closer. You're my big brother."

When his eyes lifted to meet mine, there was something there I hadn't expected to see. Remorse.

"Are those the test samples for the new perfume?"

I followed his gaze to the conference table where my father had placed the box he'd brought up with him. Clearly Evan wasn't in the mood for a big emotional conversation, and neither was I. But he'd never been one for small talk, so I'd take this conversational olive branch for what it was worth. Maybe if we could find some common ground, we could build a relationship outside of our worth to the company.

"Yes. Do you want to test them out with me? I haven't had a chance to open them yet. I'd love your opinion."

His eyes met mine, his shock evident. "My opinion?"

"Yeah. You know what Mom likes. Hopefully you can help me pick the one that you think would make her happiest."

"Sure. I can do that."

Together, we pulled out the ten vials that were inside the box. They were labeled with their predominant ingredient, and I put the floral notes together and the musky scents aside to test last. My nose had a harder time recovering between those. I went back to my desk and pulled out the small jar of coffee beans I always kept there to help clear my sense of smell between vials.

"Let's try these first." I offered Evan one of the floral vials first and then took a quick whiff after he was done.

"That reminds me of that weird piano teacher I had in eighth grade. Remember her?"

An image of an older woman with bright purple, cat-eye glasses made me laugh. "She used to sneak sips from her flask when she thought no one was looking!"

Evan's laughter rumbled out of his chest, and he put a hand over the vial. "Not this one. I don't need anything giving me flashbacks of that summer. I hated playing the piano after smelling all that lavender perfume for an hour straight every Wednesday."

With a smile, I put the vial into a clear plastic baggie. "Okay that one is definitely out."

After fifteen minutes of going back and forth between the samples, we were able to narrow it down to four vials. There was a quick knock on the door before Oskar stuck his head in.

"We need to leave soon so we aren't late to the airport." He nodded politely at Evan.

"The airport?" Evan glanced over at me with his eyebrows raised.

"Priya is coming to visit. We're going to have such a good time. I'll bring her by your office to say hello sometime while she's here."

He grinned. "Yeah, definitely do that. I haven't seen her crazy ass in a long time."

"Evan?"

He paused and turned back around.

"Thanks for your help tonight. It was nice to just hang out. We should do it more often. I meant it when I said I wished we were closer. One day, when Mom and Dad are gone, you're going to be my only family."

A strange look passed over his face, and he stared at me for a long time. Finally, he nodded. "Yeah. We're family."

Then he was gone.

Before I could dissect my brother's odd behavior, Oskar appeared in the doorway again. "Ready to go?"

For a moment, I wanted to confide in him. I wished I could tell him all about my day, my fight with my dad, and my rare moment of connection with my brother. But then I remembered everything that had happened between us and that I was kind of still angry with him.

I nodded and then grabbed my bag. "Yes. I don't want to keep Priya waiting. If you think I'm a firecracker when I get worked up, just wait. You haven't seen anything yet."

CHAPTER SIXTEEN

Oskar

The ride to the airport was quiet. Too quiet.

My fingers clenched around the steering wheel. I was determined not to say anything and to let Hailey work through things on her own. She had the right to be a little pissed. Hell, I was too, and talking had never seemed to get us very far.

Usually it just got us to the nearest bed.

But I couldn't pretend her silent treatment didn't hurt. Hailey had finally started to open up to me again, and I'd come to cherish those moments at the end of the day when we'd unwind together. Anyone looking in might think that we were just a case of mega-lust exploding again after years apart, but they didn't know how my restlessness calmed as soon as I saw her. They didn't know how happy it made me just to see her smile or laugh. She'd become my touchstone at the end of the day, the thing that made me feel like I was at home.

Now I was cut off again, and I wasn't used to being out in the cold.

Finally, I couldn't take it anymore. Even if it got me cussed out, I'd rather that instead of riding in torturous silence for the entire car trip.

"So, tell me about Priya. She's your best friend?"

Hailey shrugged. "We've known each other a long time."

When she didn't volunteer anything else, I forced my attention back to the road. We'd left after work to pick up her friend from the airport but there was still traffic. There was always traffic in New York, but this was worse than I'd expected. I had a vision of us being stuck and me letting her down once again. It was a surprise how much the thought of that hurt.

Hailey and I were like two ships that kept crashing into each other. Fate seemed to have an absurd sense of humor.

Either that or someone upstairs was having a lot of fun pranking us. But no matter what, the truth was we were being thrown together for a reason. She was a part of my past I'd mistakenly assumed was over, but clearly there was more in store for the two of us. We were both adults and should be able to figure this thing out instead of ignoring it.

"Look, I know the marriage thing took us both by surprise, but a divorce will be easy considering the circumstances."

Hailey swiveled in her seat, her eyes filled with murder. No, seriously, if murder was an expression, it was all over her face.

"Easy?" Even though she didn't raise her voice, the tone easily conveyed a quiet but deadly message.

"Uh, yeah. I mean, it's just paperwork, really."

Man. I'd thought she looked homicidal before, but her expression right then made me want to pull the car over and get out for my own safety. That was the problem with women. Even when you thought you were making logical sense, they could still find a reason to want to tie your balls in a knot.

"Divorce is not a joke to me. I know you don't respect

marriage, but I do." Hailey turned around in her seat to face out the window, completely freezing me out.

Whoa. She wasn't just pissed about the inconvenience of discovering an unknown legal hassle. I realized in that moment that I'd read her completely wrong. This wasn't even about the embarrassment of finding out just how drunk and stupid we'd been that weekend. For Hailey, this was something more. Something sacred. And I'd treated it like a joke.

"It wasn't my intention to make light of the situation. Or to be flippant. I hate seeing you so upset, so I thought going straight to a solution would help. I just want to see you smile again."

Being so caught off guard, I found myself admitting things I never would have otherwise. Hell, I didn't even know if I'd admitted that to myself yet. But it was the truth.

My world was pretty simple at this point. If Hailey was happy, then so was I. But if she wasn't, God help us all.

Hailey pinched the bridge of her nose. "I know you didn't mean it. We just have different ideas about what constitutes a solution here. Because the word *divorce* isn't ever going to make me smile."

We'd reached the exit for the airport, and I had to take a hard right to make it. The next few minutes were occupied with finding the right gate and then maneuvering for a parking space in the loading area.

"We're right on time," Hailey remarked. "Thanks for driving me. I didn't want her to have to take a cab."

"Of course." Even though I responded automatically, I realized how true it was. I was happy to do things for Hailey because she always made me feel appreciated. Even when we were fighting, it was obvious that she just wanted us both to be okay and have what we needed. She didn't take any crap and expected the best from me. It was a totally new experience to have a woman expect things from me that made me a better person. Hailey didn't need me to buy her anything. She needed me to be a good person that she could rely on. It was a huge eye-opener and also a privilege. She was exactly the kind of woman any man would be lucky to call his wife.

And you are that lucky man.

It was a sobering thought.

Hailey got out of the car and before I could follow, I heard a chorus of shrieking. *What the hell?* I threw open the door, one hand going instinctively to my holstered weapon. But it wasn't a threat. Instead it was two huge clouds of dark, curly hair bouncing around together as they hugged and screamed. I wasn't sure how they managed to make that much noise while holding on to each other, but my eardrums could testify that it was happening.

"Let's continue this reunion in the car. I don't like you being exposed like this."

At my words, the two broke apart and both women turned to glare at me. Priya was petite with long, dark hair and skin a few shades lighter than Hailey's, hinting at possible Indian ancestry. Her dark eyes locked on me with interest.

"Damn girl, you didn't lie. Big, bossy Viking has spoken."

Unsure of how to respond to that, I finally just leaned down and grabbed her suitcase that had been knocked over in all the commotion.

"Oskar, this is my best friend Priya. Priya, this is Oskar. He's my bodyguard and a huge pain in the ass."

Priya smirked. "A pain in the ass, huh? Well, sometimes pain can be pleasure. Nice to meet you."

"Nice to meet you too, Priya. Now, let's go."

She pursed her lips before opening the back door. "I don't normally take direction well, but I'll make an exception. I have a feeling this weekend will be worth it."

***

Hailey

Riding back to the penthouse, it was a miracle that Priya didn't bore a hole in the back of my head before we got there. I could almost feel the questions bubbling up in her mind. I would be lucky if I could get her behind a closed door and away from Oskar's ears before she let loose.

Wait until she found out where we were staying.

"So, we're not going to my place. I'm staying somewhere else temporarily for security reasons." I turned around to see Priya grinning at the back of Oskar's head.

"Uh-huh." She raised her eyebrows and then glanced at him again. "Security reasons, huh?"

"Yeah. I'll explain later."

I whipped around before she could ask any other questions. But she was quiet until we turned into the underground garage at Blake Security. When Oskar got out of the car to get the luggage, Priya grabbed the back of my seat as soon as his door closed.

"You have a lot of explaining to do. Where are we? It looks like some underground bunker in the movies."

We both got quiet when Oskar opened her door and then mine. As we walked behind him, I knew she wasn't missing how alert Oskar was, his eyes constantly moving around the garage. When he put his hand on the palm scanner to activate the elevator, Priya elbowed me in the ribs.

"Lot of explaining to do," she whispered.

When the elevator doors opened, we stepped out into the lobby. Priya nodded approvingly. "Nice place."

Oskar checked his phone. "Guest room five is open. Come on. I'll show you where it is."

We followed him past the kitchen and down the hallway that led to the extra bedrooms. Each door was had a different ornate decal, something I hadn't noticed before.

Probably too busy ogling a certain hunky Viking.

"This is where I'm staying." I pointed at number the door

next to hers. "I'm so glad you're here. It feels like it's been forever."

"Yes, it does. And clearly we have a lot to catch up on." Priya turned to look at Oskar meaningfully.

I blushed. Yeah, she definitely wasn't going to let me slide at all.

Oskar shifted from foot to foot. "Uh, can we talk for a second?"

It was rare to see him caught off guard, but I could tell our earlier conversation in the car had him on edge. I was, too. The whole thing was crazy, and his reaction had upset me a lot more than I'd let on. Divorce was common now, so it wouldn't be a big deal to a lot of people, but in my family it would be a scandal. My parents would not only be disappointed but also hurt. They'd dreamed about giving me away in a big, white wedding and I felt sure hearing the news that I was getting a divorce before they even knew I was married wouldn't be easy.

Not any easier than it was for me to digest.

"This really isn't the best time. Maybe later after I've had a chance to get Priya settled in?"

But of course, my bestie being who she was couldn't wait to throw me under the bus.

"Oh, I don't need settling. Actually, I'm kind of tired." Priya gave an exaggerated yawn.

I crossed my arms. This was coming from the same woman who drank Red Bull for breakfast and had more energy than ten Chihuahuas combined.

"Tired, huh?"

Priya wouldn't meet my eyes, but there was no disguising the smile tugging at the edges of her lips. "Yes, so tired. I'll probably take a nap. A nice, long nap. So you know, you don't have to worry about me knocking on your door and interrupting anything."

Oskar snorted, and I narrowed my eyes at him. "There will be nothing to interrupt. At least let me show you to your room."

But Priya was already moving in that direction. At the last second, she doubled back and grabbed the handle of her other suitcase. "See, I've got it. You don't have to walk me down all the way. I'll just go have a quick shower and then take my nap. We can hang out later. Much later."

I sighed. Clearly I wasn't going to get out of this conversation with Oskar. Priya surely thought she was helping by making herself scarce, and there was no way I could tell her that I really didn't want to be alone with him right then without admitting that I was nervous in front of the man himself. There was no way I was giving him that kind of ammunition. It was hard enough to keep my wits about me without flat out telling him that he made it hard to concentrate.

"Okay. Just come get me when you're done."

Priya didn't respond other than an absent wave as she set off down the hall, finally stopping at the room on the end. She opened the door and then skidded to a halt. "Whoa!"

Her duffel bag thudded to the ground at her feet.

I jogged down the hall, vaguely aware of Oskar right on my heels. When I stopped right behind Priya, I immediately put a hand in front of my eyes. But it was a little late to block the image of a completely naked Tyse standing in the middle of the room.

"Damn, this place is full-service. I didn't know my room came with man candy on the pillow." Priya let loose a sharp wolf whistle.

Oskar's growl behind me would have been annoying, but

as soon as I opened my eyes and saw Tyse inching around the bed trying to cover the family jewels with a way-too-small throw pillow, I lost it, laughing hysterically.

"Sorry, Tyse. I guess we got the wrong room."

Priya resisted my efforts to tug her backward so I could close the door.

"No, I think this is the right room," she said, raising her eyebrows at Tyse.

CHAPTER SEVENTEEN

Hailey

The next evening, I knew my reprieve was almost up. After a quick scramble to find Priya another room, Oskar had gotten called into a meeting. By the annoyed look on his face I could tell he hadn't wanted to leave, but between his work and my guest, the universe had given me a get out of jail free card for the rest of the evening.

I'd spent an enjoyable day with Priya, visiting MOMA and then one of my favorite Indian restaurants. Tyse and Dylan had been with us the whole time, but we'd easily ignored them and just enjoyed being able to hang out again. Once we'd gotten back to the penthouse, Priya had gone to make some calls, so I took the opportunity to change into more comfortable clothes and check my emails. Anything to avoid thinking about the conversation I wasn't ready to have.

But it was time for dinner and I couldn't hide in my room any longer.

As soon as I opened the door, Priya appeared at the other end of the hallway.

"Finally!" she exclaimed. "I've been waiting for you. Did you have it out with big, blond, and bossy yet?"

"Not yet."

"I'm sure it won't be long if the way he was looking at you is any indication. What's up with you two? He's so intense, like he'd take a bullet for you or something."

"Well, he would. But that's his job."

Priya raised one perfectly arched eyebrow. "Is it his job to stare at your ass, too?"

"Things are so complicated. I don't even know where to start." The words were burning a hole through my tongue.

Oskar hadn't said anything about keeping our marriage under wraps, and I was in dire need of some advice just then.

"It turns out we did more than just get drunk in Vegas. Apparently, we also visited one of those tacky wedding chapels."

We were coming to the end of the hallway, and my words made Priya stumble into the wall. She turned around to glare at me. "Are you freaking kidding me?"

Her voice was loud enough to have everyone else in the room looking over at us.

"Whoa, ladies. Is everything all right?"

Tyse's deep voice cut between us. It took a minute before I could get myself together enough to answer.

"Just fine. Thanks."

He asked the question of both of us, but his eyes were still on Priya. She accepted his outstretched hand as we walked into the kitchen where Lucia and JJ were peering into a large pot.

"What are you guys making?" I asked before sending Priya

a warning glance. I knew she was dying right then with a million questions, but those would have to wait. I didn't want the whole house in our business. Especially since he seemed so excited about the possibility of divorcing before anyone found out.

I ignored the wave of hurt the thought brought back. He wasn't the marrying type, and it shouldn't be a surprise that he wasn't chomping at the bit to play house with a woman he hadn't seen in years. Despite our insane sexual chemistry, we were only together now due to a strange twist of circumstances not because he'd missed me or had sought me out. I had come to terms with his disappearance from my life back then and certainly hadn't been pining for him since.

Random dreams about that weekend didn't count.

"So how long are you staying, Priya?" Tyse asked after pulling out one of the barstools at the granite counter for her to sit. "Once Hailey goes back to work, do you need a tour guide?"

Tyse was watching her so closely that even I shivered from the intensity. As usual, Priya spoke her thoughts aloud for everyone to hear.

She leaned toward Tyse. "With the way you're staring at me, I guess that means *you're* volunteering to help me with *all* of my needs?"

Oskar appeared out of nowhere and shoved Tyse aside. "Don't worry Priya. Our guests aren't on the menu."

"Speak for yourself," Tyse muttered.

Oskar scowled. "Stop looking at her like you're hunting. I know how you assassin types are."

"Assassin types?" Priya glanced over at me. I shrugged.

Tyse smirked, but Oskar looked a little uncomfortable. "Just an inside joke," he reassured her.

But something about the harsh set of his jaw told me there was way more to the story than that.

"I need friends like that," Priya commented. "If y'all are taking people out, I have a few candidates I can add to the list."

Tyse stopped laughing. "Boyfriend bothering you?"

Priya scoffed. "I don't keep them long enough to call them boyfriends."

"Well, if they don't know how to behave all I need is a name."

Geez, what was it with these guys? They could go from frat boy to killer in the blink of an eye.

"I'll keep that in mind." Priya was looking at him like she wouldn't mind Tyse bothering her. Not at all.

Oh boy. I knew my best friend and when she got that look in her eye, any red-blooded man didn't stand a chance. I hoped Tyse was as aggressive as he appeared. He'd need to be or Priya would chew him up and spit him out before her visit was over.

Oskar leaned into my side. I ignored the familiar zing of arousal I got whenever he was near.

"Are you ready to talk now? Or are you going to invent another excuse to avoid me?"

I sighed. Priya was clearly capable of holding her own, and we really did need to talk things through. Like it or not, we were married, and ignoring it wouldn't make it go away.

"No, we can talk now. Might as well get it over with."

Oskar

I followed the sway of Hailey's hips as she walked back down the hallway to my room.

Might as well get it over with.

That didn't bode well for the fate of this conversation. The muted laughter of the others behind us was a stark contrast to the tense set of her shoulders.

"So, are you still mad at me?"

She rolled her eyes. "I never said I was mad at you. This is not the kind of situation where I can really blame you for it. We both signed the marriage license so if I'm angry, it's with both of us."

I leaned back against the door, watching her as she paced across the carpet. "I have to say, it seemed like you were mad at me yesterday."

She crossed her arms. "I wasn't mad. Just disappointed. You just showed me how differently we think about marriage. This is a big deal to me."

Suddenly she stopped pacing. "Oh man, I was almost a polygamist!"

It took a second for the meaning to hit me. "You were going to marry someone? Who?"

She rolled her eyes. "That's what you're worried about right now? My last boyfriend?"

I sauntered closer. When I pulled her into my arms, she struggled slightly. But in the end, she let out a little huff and buried her head in my chest.

"Yeah, I'm worried about it. The thought that someone else had the right to touch you drives me crazy," I muttered, fully aware that I was making no sense.

Hailey's fist landed in my gut, and I chuckled.

"It's not funny, Oskar. You left me. And Steven was there for me. You weren't."

Her angry eyes made me feel like I was being punched all over again. The worst part was that she was right. I was the dipshit who'd left, and this other guy had been there to take care of her when I wasn't.

"He's not here now. I'm here, and I'm not going to let anyone else near you again." My control finally ran out and I had to taste her again.

She moaned when our lips connected. The fingers that had been pushing at my chest clenched and clung, tugging my shirt as she held on. Together we moved backward until we bumped up against the bed, but our mouths stayed fused together, tasting all the regret we shared between us. But it was more than just old feelings that kept my lips traveling over her cheek then down to her neck. It was more than just jealousy that made me pick her up and squeeze the luscious little ass that she loved to wiggle and tempt me with.

It was the knowledge that we were now tied together. Despite my best efforts to push her away all those years ago, fate had thrown us back together anyway. All the emotion I'd tried to avoid had boomeranged back and clocked me right upside the head.

Buoyed by her hot eyes on my body, I yanked my shirt over my head and threw it to the ground.

The look of lust on her face was going to be my favorite fantasy for years to come. How she could amp me up with one look, I would never understand, but that was my Hailey.

And she was mine.

"You belong to me. Every inch of you." I mumbled the words as my lips crushed against hers and tasted. I was being too rough, but any thoughts of slowing down flew away when Hailey leaned up and sucked my lower lip between her teeth.

"Does that mean this is mine, too?" she asked wistfully, running her hands all over my chest.

"Hell yeah, it does. It always has been."

"Always? You have some fucking nerve to say that to me when I didn't even know where you were until a few weeks ago!"

Her anger was justified, but her assumption that I was off living some carefree life rankled.

"Do you really think that's what I wanted? That if I'd had a choice, I would have left you behind in that hotel room instead of crawling back into bed next to you?"

"If you wanted that, then why didn't you at least try to stick it out?"

With a groan, I hung my head. Even now, I couldn't be fully honest with her, and it sucked. "I wanted to. I still want that."

My words brought her eyes up, and something passed between us in that moment, something too big and too complicated to examine just yet, so I stepped back and unzipped my jeans. Hailey's eyes fell to my waist. Her lids lowered as she examined the bulge in the front of my jeans and then she smiled, that wicked grin that always preceded trouble.

"Why do I feel this way when I know you're just going to hurt me again?"

I thought she was going to get up right then and leave me behind. She was probably better off if she did. But instead, she leaned forward and kissed the skin right above my waistband. The wet heat of her lips against my skin was the last straw.

"Fuck, Hailey. If you don't want this, tell me now."

Her fingers grasped the sides of my jeans and tugged them down. "I want this. And this time you're going to be the one left begging for more."

Anything I was going to say was cut off when she pulled my boxers down next. I would have expected her to be gentle and dainty. The Hailey I'd known before, while a firecracker, had also been reserved and unsure in bed at first. But this Hailey was not waiting around for direction. She dipped her head and her lips closed around my cock, making me cry out. Then she hummed like she'd finally gotten a treat she'd been waiting for. That hum was the sexiest thing.

"Oh shit. Baby, wait."

Now I sounded like the innocent, trying to slow things down. But Hailey was lost in her own world, teasing and tempting as her soft lips roamed over my skin while her hands did the same. I was lost in her and didn't want to be found. Taking her hand, I tugged her to the bed and tumbled down pulling her to me. I pulled her up for a kiss and when she straddled me, I almost saw stars.

"How did I survive without this for so long?"

She shook her head. "I don't know. Only you know that. I just hope one day you trust me enough to tell me."

The guilt swamped me again but then all thought was lost as she sank down, taking all of me into her warmth. Her eyes were still angry, but she leaned down to kiss me, a harsh, punishing kiss that told me she was going to take her anger out on my body. Everything was all fucked up, but the one thing that had always been perfect was our connection. Nothing could ever take away the perfection we found when we touched.

Her head fell back as she moved her hips, and in that moment, I knew that I was a goner. I had never felt like this with any other woman and I never would again.

I was in love with Hailey Livingston.

CHAPTER EIGHTEEN

Hailey

I watched Priya watching Tyse watch her. The two of them were seriously eye fucking. And neither one of them was trying to hide it. When my best friend stood up from the game of Rummy 500, and very casually and slowly walked by Tyse, the poor guy couldn't help but track her every move. Full-on intensity, like he wanted to rip her clothes off and tear her to pieces. Or, well, tear all her clothes off and lick her to pieces, whichever.

Either way, she'd be naked. I grabbed Oskar's empty beer and headed toward the kitchen with her.

He looked up from his cards and he winked at me. Silly or not, I flushed. A simple little thing and just like that, he could make me warm and soft and need him. Priya was right. He had the key to orgasms. Specifically, *my* orgasms. I didn't even know how he knew what to do, but I was blissfully chilled out. Well, as chilled out as *I* could be.

"You know what you're doing, right?"

Priya dragged her head out of the refrigerator and smiled. "What do you mean?"

"With Tyse? You know what you're doing."

She giggled. "Oh, you mean the foreplay?"

"Are you sure that's what that is? Because the guy looks like he's ready to pounce on you."

"Good. That's exactly how I want him to look. "

"Okay, fine. I get it. But you know, just be careful. These guys are... intense? That's not even the right word because they're so much more than intense."

"Seriously, you need to stop worrying." Priya stood, marched over to me, and clasped her hands on my shoulders. "I don't even live here. This thing with Tyse is just fun. It's a game. None of this is real. But even if it were real, that's what I want, someone intense. Sexy."

"Okay, if you say so."

After all, I wasn't her mother. I checked my phone again. Waiting, checking for the email I'd been waiting on for the last three hours.

"If you check your phone one more time, I swear to God I'm going to open my mouth and scream out, 'Intruder'. Then we'll have a half-dozen men up here in two seconds."

I put down my phone. "Happy?"

Priya shrugged. "Marginally."

"Sorry, I'm just thinking about the gala. I want everything to be perfect."

"It will be perfect for your mom. She'll know the meaning behind it, and that's all that matters." She shook out her hair. "Now that we've got all that deep emotional shit out of the way, please tell me you've been with Captain Viking and that it was amazing. I'm sure you have, because you're not walking right, but I need you to give me details because his hands..."

Priya mimicked what she assumed would be the gargantuan size of Oskar's dick with her hands. Truth be told, she wasn't *that* far off.

I giggled. "I can't believe you."

"I mean, come on. Tell me *something*. This is like hot-guy central, and they could use some more estrogen up in here. You should totally keep boning the Viking and let him give you little brown Viking babies, but if you're not up for it, I will fall on that sword. You know, not *his* sword because you're my girl, but any other sword in here. I volunteer as tribute."

I laughed so hard I snorted. It really was a sword if I was being honest. I grabbed Oskar a beer and looped my arm through hers. She was exactly what I needed at that crazy time. She was completely insane, of course, but I loved her, and she was mine. I couldn't believe that I got to spend the next few days with her.

It felt good having someone to talk to about all the Oskar stuff. I needed someone to give it to me straight tell me like it was.

Without her, I might have still been playing it safe.

Oskar

I should have been paying attention at the status meeting, and I was... *half* paying attention. My laptop was open. I was scowling at the spread-sheets, as I was known to do. I *looked* like I was paying attention. That must count for something.

Instead, I was staring at Hailey.

At just the thought of her, my dick was ready for action, as if she'd physically touched me. How the hell was that possible?

Matthias was saying something. "With the bad news... debt..."

I dragged my attention back to what was happening.

"What was that?"

Matthias frowned at me. "Evan is in debt up to his eyeballs." He pushed a written report across the table to me.

I whistled low as I read it. Holy shit. The majority of shares were held by Hailey's father, while her mother had only a small percentage. The rest had been split between

Hailey and her brother. But Evan, the dumb prick, had apparently gambled away the majority of his shares.

Noah sighed. "Okay, let's not disclose this to Hailey yet. Even if he's in debt, we don't have any proof that Evan is behind anything. Let's keep this quiet until we can prove whether he has anything to do with her case."

I nodded. "Clients usually don't react well when you accuse family members, so we need some evidence."

Noah slanted me a glance. "You know I'm saying this for you, right?"

I scowled. "What do you mean?"

Noah just rolled his eyes. "No pillow talk. This is confidential."

I ground my teeth. Then my attention was caught by the sight of Hailey walking by the door again. And there went my dick one more time. I was happy she had Priya here.

Watching her with Priya, I could see her friend dragged her out of her shell the same way I did. Priya was completely outrageous. Even more so than JJ, and that was saying something.

JJ was one of my favorite people on the planet. Mostly

because she said all the inappropriate things I couldn't get away with.

Noah snapped his fingers. "Hey, are you listening?"

"Yeah, I heard you. No pillow talk, confidential, don't tell Hailey anything about her idiot brother. I got it."

The guys all traded glances. I just pretended like I couldn't see them.

Jonas cleared his throat. "Yeah, so glad we covered that because the next order of business is security for the gala."

I scowled at him. Jonas held his hands up. "Don't look at me, man. It's on the agenda."

"She's not going."

Rafe coughed a laugh. "Did you tell her that yet?"

I ground my teeth. "There's nothing to tell. She's just not going."

Jonas snickered. "Oh, Rafe, do you want to tell him?"

Rafe laughed. "No, I'm not going to tell him. The kid should tell him."

Matthias just blinked and stared wide-eyed at everyone. "Oi, why do I have to tell him?"

Noah sighed. "Ugh, pussies. I'll tell him."

I scowled at the lot of them, wishing they didn't know I was generally good-natured. The Viking scowl usually worked on everybody.

"What aren't you telling me?"

Noah sighed. "Remember that time before Lucia and I got together? How I used to tell her what to do, and that never ended well for me?"

"Yeah? You were a dick."

Noah coughed as he laughed. "Much like you are now. Remember how I ran around here making decisions without talking to her? Do you remember what happened to me then?"

I thought back. Oh yeah, Lucia had been pissed. "Hailey is different. She's even-tempered. Rational."

Everyone at the table laughed then. Even Tyse.

I scowled at the kid. "What the fuck are you laughing at?"

"Hey, I may be a cold-blooded former assassin, but even I know you are an idiot."

"What? She's going to understand the rationale behind it. It's too dangerous."

Rafe clapped me on the back as he stood. "It's been nice knowing you." Then he glanced around the room. "Bet you all a C-note that she cuts off his left nut first."

Jonas shook his head. "Nah, I reckon she'll wax his balls first, then slit his throat."

Matthias just shook his head. "Neither of you are right, mates. She's going to go all cold and calculating and then plot his demise. She's going to get the girls in on it, and then JJ is going to start ordering lye online. It's going to get ugly from there."

Everyone turned to him and stared.

He shrugged. "What? Too dark?"

Rafe shook his head. "No bio-disposal talk in the conference room, man. It makes some of us nervous."

Sure enough, me, Jonas, Ryan and Dylan all looked a little queasy at the mention of lye. Ryan and Dylan didn't know all the down and dirty, but they knew that Noah, Rafe, Tyse, and Matthias had been into some bad shit. And the more that leaked out, the clearer the picture became.

Matthias groaned. "All I'm saying is Hailey will make you hurt. Then she's going to get her mates in on it. And then none of us are going to get any."

Everyone groaned around the table. "Dude, don't fuck with my good thing," Rafe muttered.

Jonas just shrugged. "I'm still in my honeymoon phase. She'll be mad, but she won't cut me off."

Noah groaned. "Lucia won't cut me off, but it might take some convincing depending on how mad she is." He slid me a glance and sighed. "Whatever this is, talk to her before you go deciding things. If my wife goes on strike because of you being a dumbass, I'll kill you."

I snarled at him. "You're welcome to try."

Most people would have been terrified by that. But not Noah. *No.* That motherfucker just grinned. I had a feeling he welcomed that dare. Maybe it was a good idea to talk to her. She would, of course, see it as rational. These guys were wrong. She would absolutely listen to me. After all, I was right.

CHAPTER NINETEEN

Hailey

"What the hell did you just say?"

Oskar rolled his shoulders. My body went soft and giddy and wet, just with a small movement. I knew what those shoulders could do. He'd surprised me at work just yesterday and shown me quite a few things that muscular body could do, even in the cramped space of a supply closet.

Do not get distracted. He just said you can't go to the gala.

He put his hands up. "Listen, butterfly, it's just—"

"Do *not* call me butterfly. I've been working my whole

career for this. This is a huge deal. This perfume will change everything." *Way to put a lot of pressure on yourself.* "And you just stand there and tell me I can't go?"

He winced. "Okay, that was a misuse of words. I'm saying it's a bad idea for you to go."

"So, I can go then?"

His lips pressed into a firm line. "No. If I had to choose, I'd choose you not going because I'm trying to keep you alive."

I resisted the urge to throw my letter opener at him.

My father cleared his throat. "Sweetheart, I don't mean to interfere, but we hired Blake Security for a reason. Let's think this through."

"You're siding with him?" I narrowed my gaze at my father, who, to his credit, didn't back down.

"Sweetheart, I care about this perfume. We've put a lot of money in it. You know I have believed in you every single step of the way. But keeping you safe is more important than any gala. The perfume will be a success either way. Quite frankly, we'll seem more mysterious if we cancel. Everyone will be clamoring to know what happened and insist on trying it. So in a way, it will be more of a success if we *don't* have a gala."

My father looked so pleased with his justification. I threw up my hands.

More successful? All the work I'd put in, and everyone just wanted to scrap it and move on? No matter how my dad tried to spin this, it wouldn't be more successful to skip the gala.

Because then my mother wouldn't see how hard I'd worked on it.

I crossed my arms and glared at Oskar. All I wanted was one perfect night to show my mom how much I loved her. And no one was going to take that away from me.

Oskar

I couldn't believe it. They were right. Telling her she couldn't go to the gala had been the wrong move. As a matter of fact, I was pretty sure she was eyeing her letter opener to see if she could throw it at me.

She glanced at Noah, who sat stoically. "It's your call."

"Do you see that? Your boss says it's my call."

I could barely contain the growl toward Noah. "I'm just saying it's prudent for you not to have the gala."

Why was she being so stubborn? "Hailey, you now live at the penthouse because somebody sideswept us. Somebody scared you in your own apartment. Somebody tried to grab you at the boutique. Are you kidding me right now?"

Her eyes sent daggers my way. From the corner, her brother scoffed. "Jesus Christ. Let her go to the damn gala. Even *I* can see how important this is to her."

I glared at him. "Really Evan? Now is the time for you to act like her brother?"

Even Hailey was surprised. "You're siding with me, Evan?"

"Yeah, I'm siding with you. You and I don't always get along, but at the end of the day, you work your ass off. You should get to celebrate it. Besides, you know I love a good party."

I rolled my eyes. "Look Hailey, it's just safer if you don't do this."

"Well, safer or not, I've put too much work into this. Blood, sweat, and tears. I have a whole team who worked to make this happen. This is for my mother—" She cut herself off midway through and then sniffed. "You know what, I'm having the gala. It's your job to figure out how to make it safe."

And then she marched out, back stiff, pride stung. I hated seeing her like that.

The meeting broke up then. Her father, presumably, was going to try and talk some sense into her. Evan was going to do whatever it was Evan did. Hopefully, not gamble away more money. Matthias pulled me aside as I walked everyone out.

"Follow me."

I frowned as I followed the kid down the hall, and then to the left to his set of rooms.

"What's wrong?"

If he pulled me aside here, it meant there was something I needed to see that he didn't want anyone else knowing or overhearing.

"Just something that you need to see."

I stared at his monitors. "I don't know what I'm looking at here. Help me out."

He pointed at a spot. "These are the birth records for Hailey's mother. See anything unusual?"

I did. *Holy shit.* Things were going to get a whole lot worse before they got better.

Hailey

God, this one pinched.

It just wasn't made for a woman with curves. Any kind of ass was a problem with this silver-sequined number.

"I don't know. It doesn't look right."

"Honey, this is the fourth gown you have tried on that you were like, 'ahh, I don't know, my butt looks weird.' You are the one who left the sexy Viking out there. I'm sure he'd have *all* the opinions on these. Mostly, I'm like, 'They look pretty. They make your tits look good.'"

I scowled at her. "I need real opinions. I need to look regal, but beautiful, but also slightly reserved. And sexy."

Priya tossed up her hands. "That's a tall order, baby. How about hot? Can I just say hot?"

"How is it you don't like shopping? I mean, everything else about you is so BFF."

Priya shrugged. "I'm just not patient. If you bring me a personal stylist who has picked everything up for me and I only have to make two choices, then I'm a happy camper. Otherwise, I'm just like, 'I don't know, the red one? As long as it makes my tits look good.'"

"You're impossible."

"Honey, you do realize that Oskar is the one who should be telling you how your ass looks in these dresses, right?"

I rolled my eyes. "Well, you can have him if you need a big block of concrete to give you an opinion."

"Babes, I love you, I just—I don't know. Maybe you're being a little hard on him?"

I pivoted slowly to glare at her, but she wasn't having it. "No, you don't. You don't turn that cold stare on me. I'm not going to shrivel up and hope to die praying that maybe you'll look away and won't notice that I fucked something up. I'm telling you like it is. I love you, full stop. I also think you're being too hard on him. He's just saying what we're all thinking."

I crossed my arms. "Oh, what we're all thinking?"

"Yeah, I'm on your side, babe. The side of you being safe and happy. Weren't you just telling me how happy you've been the last few weeks with him and how sweet he is?"

I hated that she was being rational. "Well now he's just a jerk. Telling me what to do, disrupting my whole life without even asking. With not a single care to how much my life is upset by this."

"Then talk to him. You can't just shut him out. Closing yourself off to feeling things doesn't work, not when you want to be with someone."

I grumbled. "Well, I'm not sure I want to be with him, anyway."

Priya stared. "Please, girl. I see the way you vanish in the middle of the day. I came by the office the other day to see you. They said you were out for lunch, but your car was still there. Hunky bodyguard number seven was looking around, so I knew you were in the office. Imagine my surprise when I walked by what must have been a supply closet, and I could hear Oskar groaning your name. And all I could think was, 'Yes, girl, yes, get you some,' because you have spent too much of your life uptight. Never having any fun."

I flushed thinking about just what we'd gotten up to in that supply closet. I cleared my throat.

"I do more than work, you know. I have fun."

Not really.

It wasn't my fault, exactly. Ever since I was a little girl, I'd been taught to focus on my studies because I'd be a part of running the family business one day. My father had always been very busy, but he'd made time to bring me to work. To me, that *had* been fun. Especially when he had new perfume samples that I could smell.

For us, it was bonding time. And well, my mother wasn't sober a lot of the time, so it hadn't always been safe to leave me with her.

"In the couple of days I've been here, I've seen how open you are and willing to have an adventure. One that's not all completely planned out to the hilt. And you've been smiling a lot. I love to see that. For a long time, you've been sad. And I know you were sad when Oskar left, but you were even sadder with Steven. You were settling, and you knew it. But you were doing it anyway because you thought that's all you deserved. But I'm watching you happy now. *He* makes you happy. So maybe cut him some slack so you guys can figure this out."

"I was happy before."

Priya gave me the *are you serious* look. "Okay, if you say so. I'm going to go get a drink, and I'll also shake my ass in front of Tyse to see if I can entice him at all. Can you believe I have been walking around here in tight, skimpy clothing, and he hasn't noticed?"

"Oh, he's noticed. He's just showing a lot of restraint."

Priya rolled her eyes. "Well, I want to see if I can break that restraint. Do you need anything?"

I shook my head and assessed myself and the gown again. Maybe I was being too rigid. My pride wasn't really worth losing the way I'd felt for the last few weeks. I had felt more alive. Kind of like Vegas, like an awakening of this person inside I didn't even know existed.

Well, that and you can't let a Viking club of that size go to waste. Yeah, I probably would feel better after a couple of orgasms, and then we could talk.

CHAPTER TWENTY

Hailey

I was on edge.

The past few days had been tumultuous, but tonight was the night. The moment where everything came together.

Last night, after we'd fought and made love and fought again, I'd gone looking for him, but he'd been in some secret meeting with Matthias. I'd waited for him to come to bed, but he never did. Then, well, I'd been too irritated to sleep with him anyway.

Pride goeth before the fall.

Damn him. I was mad, so I didn't want to want him. But I did. Luckily, I'd had my hands full most of the day, so there hadn't been much free time for thinking about him. I'd been in full preparation for tonight, but I'd expected to hear something from Oskar. A word, a text—hell, a smoke signal—to tell me if he was really going to stop me or not.

It had been Tyse who told me that I would be able to go to the gala, which was great because I planned to go anyway. If Oskar planned to stop me, he was going to have to do it physically.

That could be fun.

As a side note, I was still frustrated as hell. Like my whole body was one giant throb. After I'd finally decided that we could cure that last fight with some orgasms, going to bed without them had irritated me. But more importantly, I wanted to talk to him. I wanted to have his arms wrapped around me, and I wanted to be able to breathe. Because in his arms was the only place I felt like I could do that.

It was time for the gala to begin, and I hadn't seen him all day. I had finally settled on the low-cut silver dress that fluttered every time I moved. It wasn't the most daring choice, just daring for *me*. It made me feel like a fairy princess.

As I was leaving my room, Lucia came running down the stairs. "Hey, don't forget these."

She handed me a pair of slim, silver earrings encrusted with diamonds. "Oh my God, they're beautiful. I can't."

"Of course you can. I grabbed them from the safe this morning. Put them on."

I took out the simple studs I was wearing and put them in before I turned to face the hall mirror. "Wow. Somehow it makes everything else pop."

She grinned. "Yep, that's the idea. You look gorgeous. Why don't you head on up front. Maybe I'll get Noah to take pictures like it's prom."

I groaned. "Oh my God, is this what it's like to live with you guys all the time?"

She chuckled. "Yeah, pretty much. You're lucky JJ isn't here deciding what underwear you need to wear under that dress. Spoiler alert: she's team commando."

I coughed and laughed at the same time. "Okay, good to know."

Lucia gave me a shoulder squeeze and ran back out. A few minutes later, I could hear Izzy wailing.

Oh, poor thing. It was probably close to bedtime for her. Careful not to fall in the insanely high heels I was wearing, I walked carefully toward the living room. Then I stopped short.

Right at the end of the hallway, waiting for me, was Oskar.

"Butterfly, you look beautiful."

I drank him in. Yeah, I was staring, but the man was something else in a tuxedo. Broad shoulders, tapered waist, Jesus Lord.

He stepped forward. "I see Lucia found the earrings." He held up a delicate, diamond-encrusted, silver butterfly brooch. Gently, he pinned it to the lapel of the dress. "I can't take my eyes off of you."

I frowned. "I thought you didn't want me to go."

"Only because I want you safe in my arms where I can protect you always. That's the only reason. Otherwise, I want you to fly. I don't want to hold you back from anything. You mean too much to me."

Tears welled, and I blinked them rapidly away.

He pulled me close, and the scent of him wrapped around me, cocooning me in safety and love.

Love? I quickly shoved that away. The emotion was too strong and too deep to examine too closely. Right now, I just wanted to enjoy being in his arms again.

"You want to go to this gala. I want you to have what you want. So we're going to go, and I'm going to keep you close. At least as best I can." Then he reached down and slid my hand into his.

As simple as that. That small gesture, more than anything else, branded me as his.

Forty-five minutes later, we pulled up to the venue. Life-size versions of the perfume bottle lined the red carpet. God, it was so beautiful. Oskar opened the door for me, and my hand shook as I placed it in his. Gently, he squeezed it.

"This is your show. To me, you're already perfect. Everyone else can fuck off."

I couldn't help the giggle. It was just what I needed to hear.

We walked the red carpet, hand in hand. I wouldn't let him leave me. I didn't even give a shit what the rest of the world would think. I wanted to have my photograph taken with him. I wanted everyone to know that I was his and he was mine.

We walked in, and it was better than I could have hoped. The crystal chandeliers were almost too sparkly as they lit the room with flashes of light and glittery rainbows. There was a flood of color as women in ball gowns strutted with their heels making a *click-clack* sound on the marble. Everywhere I turned, people were clinking champagne glasses. It was beautiful.

My stomach instantly tied itself into a knot as my mother approached. I held my breath. "Mama, hi. What do you think?"

She glanced around and tittered a little. Her smile was huge, but she seemed a little unsteady on her feet.

"Mom, are you okay?"

I slid my arm under hers to steady her. I could smell it, the scent of alcohol.

It wasn't just a hint of champagne but the stench of hours-old alcohol on her breath. She'd been drinking again. Today of all days, she'd been drinking.

I'd spent weeks, months, over a year seeking approval. *Love.* Only to discover she didn't care at all.

"Yeah, it's pretty. Where is the champagne?"

"Mother," I admonished gently.

She shook me off. "It's a celebration of my darling daughter."

The way she said that word was like an epithet. My heart squeezed, but then I felt Oskar's hand on my lower back, rubbing gently. His brows furrowed. Then he mouthed the words, "Are you okay?"

I realized that with him there with me, I would be okay. And I could do something about my mother's drinking. And the first step was to get every waiter down here to cut her off. She wasn't going to be drinking anymore at my event.

She might not appreciate it now, but she would later. More importantly, I was finally looking out for my own feelings. This was my time to shine, and damn it, I was going to enjoy it to the fullest extent.

Oskar

I watched Hailey on the podium, speaking about her time at the company and the love and attention that went into Miriam, the new perfume she'd formulated. The warmth spread through my chest. God, she was absolutely incredible.

You have got it bad.

I did. I remembered what I'd said to her about our Vegas marriage. I could kick myself, honestly. I never should have said it. Divorce was the last thing on earth I wanted. Why on earth would someone like her choose someone like me? It made no sense. But after everything we'd been through, I wanted to be the person who deserved her. Or at the very least the person who could hold on to her, because I was never letting her go.

I was so in love with her.

The more I held onto that thought, more the tightness in my chest eased and warmth spread through my body. Once I stopped fighting it, it felt good. Loving her wasn't a hard thing to do. I'd probably make her crazy. Hell, it was a constant state of being. If she would have me, we'd have a real fucking wedding, with the whole crazy crew. It just might take some convincing.

Well, I'd just keep annoying her and wearing her down. She'd get there eventually. And while we waited, she could stay in my bed. I smiled to myself, thinking about the number of times I'd given her a wink or a smile, only to have her cornering me somewhere in the penthouse.

Okay, okay. So, I cornered her more often than not, but that was not the point. The point was—suddenly the hairs on my neck stood up.

I glanced over at the other guys. Rafe suddenly stood taller and had his hand on his concealed weapon more than usual. Tyse's hand immediately went to the inside of his jacket.

In my earpiece, Matthias's voice was clear. "Anyone else's spidey senses going off?"

Something wasn't right. I could feel it. My eyes tracked Hailey. She was in the middle of her speech, inviting women to come up to try a sample of Miriam. Where was her brother? Where the fuck was Evan? Her father? I pinpointed the old man easily enough. He was schmoozing. Her mother was decidedly tipsy.

The first shot rang out, and I had to go on pure instinct.

Into the com, I shouted, "Rafe! Hailey."

I was too far away, or I'd be covering her like a human shield. Luckily, Rafe was right there and dove for her onstage. He shielded her with his body and then dragged her off the stage to safety.

Good. Because I was going after the shooter. I wanted to finally nail this motherfucker.

"Matthias, what do we know?"

"East side," was his response.

Tyse and I bolted. From the entrance, I saw Jonas taking off with Dylan, and Delaney steps behind him.

From home base, Noah was calling the shots. "Matthias, give us eyes."

"I'm trying. Someone cut our feed. Not the main feed, *our* feed. Someone who knew where to look."

Noah cursed, but he wasted no time. "Rafe, tuck Hailey in the safe room. Join the others."

Rafe's voice was clear. Not even labored. But there was a tightness to it, an edge. I knew he was doing exactly what I'd asked him. He was protecting Hailey. "Ten-four."

I didn't know what was happening or why, but with everybody running and screaming, knowing Hailey was safe was the most important thing. I knew Rafe was on it. He'd handily kill anyone who so much as looked at her sideways. But I still held my breath until his voice came back on the line. "Client secure."

We'd selected the safe rooms before the gala began. Several of them actually. In case anyone had access to our protection plans, which they didn't, but in case anyone did, there were four rooms that were cleared. And we'd made the game-time decision in the van before the event, so anybody with forewarning would have to guess. And with all of us on site, no one wanted to do that and guess wrong.

As soon as I knew she was safe, my breathing eased. "Fantastic. Now let's go kill the motherfucker." Unlike the former ORUS guys, I was no assassin. I'd never even killed anyone before. But in that moment, with someone threatening the woman I loved, I found myself absolutely and completely capable of it.

Hailey

Oh God, what was happening? Was my father okay? My mom?

Rafe's voice had brooked no argument when he led me to this nondescript conference room, turned off the lights and said, "Stay put."

I knew he wasn't angry with me. He was just working. He had the same look Oskar got on his face. Tight. Pinched. Hyper-focused.

I had no choice but to pace. I could have sat, but I was too keyed up and worried. My stomach was doing flip flops. God, I just hoped everyone was okay. And the samples... *What about the samples?*

The last thing we needed was some competitor getting a hold of them. Was this corporate espionage?

Focus on what you can control.

Oh God, okay. Relax. Relax. Relax.

I shook my hands out. I paced, trying to steady my breathing and calm my mind. Freaking out was going to do me no good. When I was little, around the age of three, my mother had insisted that I needed some kind of therapist because I was so hyper all the time, always bouncing, always running around.

I needed ways to calm myself, ways to learn how to behave more appropriately. Sometimes, that inner part of me just wanted to bounce off the walls, but I always reined her in to be the perfect little girl. One *she* could love. Not that it had ever worked.

God, I wished I wasn't alone. Was everyone okay?

Unable to sit down, I pulled my phone out of my small clutch bag. I had to do something. Just sitting here was going to drive me crazy.

Swiping through the photos I'd taken over the course of the night, I tagged the ones we might want to use for marketing. There was one of my mother. She was talking to someone, smiling. For once, she actually looked happy.

Then I pulled up my presentation. While I hadn't been able to complete my speech, that didn't mean I wouldn't be able to use it for marketing purposes. I hadn't even gotten to the best part toward the end where I'd planned to show vintage images of my parents.

There two in the slideshow that I'd never seen before.

What the hell, I'd done the presentation myself. I'd sent them to my father for final approval. Had he added these? The images were in sepia, and they had the date stamped on the bottom, vintage style. Like an old timey photograph.

I laughed at my mother in her miniskirt. But I could only frown when I saw the dates. There was no way she'd looked like that then. Someone must have the date wrong. From the pictures, she should have been clearly pregnant with me. Honestly, about to pop. I lightly fingered the time stamp. These pictures were taken only three months before I was born, but my mother was as slim as ever. She appeared to be laughing as she stared up at my father.

I fixed my gaze on her belly in the photos. The timing looked right, but my birthday was three months later.

I heard a click and I whipped around. A shadowy figure came through a door that I hadn't even realized was there.

Hell, Rafe hadn't left me with a weapon. All I had was my phone, and, oh godammit, a pen. Okay, then. I grabbed the pen off the table, clicked it and stood poised for an attack.

"I'm armed."

The chuckle was soft and... familiar.

"Evan?"

As the figure stepped forward, moonlight from the skylight illuminated him. It was only then I saw the gun in his hand.

"What the hell, Evan? Why do you have a gun?" Granted, I'd been wishing for one, but the last thing I needed was for my brother to shoot someone accidentally.

He waved the gun erratically. "God, you are such a fucking princess. Always getting what you want. Even the one night you claimed was supposed to be about Mom somehow ended up being about you."

I shook my head and backed up. What the hell was happening? "Evan, I'm your sister. I love you. You used to love me so much. What happened? No matter how bad anything is, we are family. We can fix this."

Evan's chuckle was cold. He lifted his gun hand. "Funny you should mention us being family."

My heart dropped. Oh God, this was it. I wouldn't even get to say goodbye to Oskar. The next sound, the resounding click that marked the end of my fate, echoed in the small room. There was nowhere to run. There was nowhere to hide.

This was the end of the line, at the hands of my own brother.

Thank you for reading BRAZEN!

The next book, *Still Brazen*, is available at malonesquared.com/brazen

Several of the side characters in this story are from our other books. Find out more about Sebastian, the Prince of the Winston Isles and Mya Taylor, the marketing agent with the funny story!

I never wanted the **throne**...

I have a plan: find my **long-lost brother** & make him the prince so I don't have to rule.

The last thing I have time for is my **sexy new neighbor**. She's everything I don't want, sassy, funny and...*not* available.

That's okay—I'm amazing best-guy-friend material.. **Friends? Sure.** Anything more? Definitely not.

All I have to do is **not touch her, kiss her or fanta-size about**...never mind...

It's not like I have a choice. I can't let her find out who I really am. And she's got secrets of her own.

Start Reading Cheeky Royal at
nanamaloneromance.net/cheekyroyal

My cock a doodle doo is on strike.

Yeah I know, I can't believe it either. Years of perfect performance and now this traitor decides to get picky. And the only woman who gets him going is my co-worker. Rival, she-devil and my competition for the biggest ad account this side of the Atlantic.

If we want to win the hottest wedding designer in the world, we have to prove we understand his business. Love. Passion. Marriage. But it turns out Mya isn't familiar with any of the above.

When I find out she's never taken a trip to O-town, we make a little wager. Not only will I win the client, but I'll prove to her that multiple O's are not a myth.

Start Reading Beg Me at mmalonebooks.com/begme

My best friend is happily coupled up and all he asked me to do is help keep her and her friend safe. But JJ is loud, argumentative and has more sass than sense. And to protect her I might have to break the vow I made years ago.

Book 1 of The Force Duet.

One-click the next book, Force!

S he wanted to give him a heart attack.

As Jonas raced through the streets, his eyes went back to his phone again and again to follow the tracker Matthias had sent. A blinking red dot that represented the one woman who could crawl under his skin.

He turned at the next street and gunned the engine. Luckily he'd been close, so the crazy woman hadn't been walking alone for too long. She was determined to send them all into heart failure. What the hell was she thinking walking home this late by herself?

An open parking space ahead beckoned and Jonas almost took out a part of the curb as he swung into it. He jumped out and slammed the door behind him, locking the vehicle with his key fob. He'd deliberately aimed for a street ahead of her so he could intercept her. Not that she'd appreciate his forethought at all. No. He fully expected to get an earful and a sassy string of expletives from the always delightful Jessica Jones.

He didn't have to wait long. She was about ten feet away and still hadn't noticed him, another thing he'd be sure to spank her ass for later. Hadn't he taught her the importance of being aware of your surroundings? But JJ was in a world of her own, her hips swinging as she strode down the street. It was only as she got closer and he saw her face that he realized this wasn't just JJ flouting the rules for fun. Her eyes were wild and darted around her frantically. She was clutching her bag to her side, not so much like she was afraid someone would steal it, but like she just needed to hold on to something.

She wasn't breaking the rules. She was scared. Something had sent her running, and Jonas needed to know what it was.

Jonas didn't move so she almost crashed into him.

"Watch it, asshole!"

He grabbed her arm and they struggled for a moment. "JJ, calm down. It's me."

Her eyes locked onto him, and for a moment she looked so vulnerable that it broke his heart. "Baby girl, it's me. Matthias sent me your coordinates when he saw you leave work without an escort."

She nodded frantically then glanced behind her. "I had to go. I just needed to get out of there."

"Okay, well, we can go wherever you need to."

His words, meant to calm, seemed to enrage her. She pointed her finger at him, getting annoyingly close to his eyes.

"I know I can go where I need to. That's what I'm doing. I don't need a man to tell me where I can go. Nobody controls me!"

Jonas threw up his hands. "No one said you couldn't. I'm trying to help you. Do you know how reckless this was, walking out alone? Anything could have happened to you, crazy woman!"

JJ clutched her bag tighter. "I've walked home plenty of times by myself before."

"I don't think you need me to tell you that things are different now."

The words took the wind out of her sails. JJ sagged a little, her eyes meeting his directly.

"Yeah. I know."

He fell into step beside her, happy when she followed him back to where he'd parked the car. Their usual routine was for one of the guys to escort her home from the office. If she needed to stay late, like she had tonight, she would call them when she was ready to go and someone would pick her up. Ever since everything had gone down last year, when her best friend had been stalked, JJ had seemed to understand how serious this all was and had cooperated with their efforts to keep her protected.

What had happened tonight to change that? Jonas wasn't sure what was going on but there had to have been something to send her fleeing into the night looking as haunted as she had earlier.

He held the door open for her and waited as she climbed up into the vehicle. She settled her bag on her lap and then turned to grab the seatbelt. When she saw him still standing in the doorway to the car, she hesitated.

"Is everything okay?"

"Do I look okay to you?" When she recoiled at his harsh tone, Jonas took a deep breath. "Sorry. No. I'm not okay. Not at all."

Jonas didn't offer any other explanation, just shut the door and walked around to the driver's side. Let her stew on that. Maybe then she'd see what it felt like to be left out in the dark, wondering what the hell was going on.

Right before he reached the driver's side door, he stopped. He was angry. Not just annoyed or peeved, but truly angry. Because whatever had scared JJ badly enough to have her running out without a word to her security was something that she hadn't come to him about. That didn't feel right at all. As much as they bickered, did JJ really not know that he'd drop whatever he was doing to help her?

He took a deep breath before opening the door and getting behind the wheel. JJ looked over at him. What he was feeling must have been broadcast on his face because she groaned.

"I don't want to hear the lecture right now, okay? I was busy at work and just felt like going home without calling out the cavalry, okay?"

Jonas shook his head, unbelievably disappointed. Not just because she wasn't taking her own safety seriously but also at the boldfaced lie. Did she really think he was that unobservant? It was an insult to him, not just as a security agent but as a man. He saw everything about her. She loved Lucia like a sister and put up with her best friend's fussing, even though she hated to be hovered over. She liked to watch Oskar lifting weights, much to Jonas's annoyance and jealousy.

He knew that she had a serious love affair with vodka. She had a hate affair with men and always chose badly.

Including the dipshits she dated who didn't even bother to pick her up at home.

So why would she think he wouldn't see through such an obvious lie?

"I'm not going to give you a lecture, JJ. Just a reminder. If shit goes bad, we can't help you if we don't know where you are."

Jonas had expected her to have a scathing response or to tell him where to stick it. But what JJ did next was the absolute last thing he'd ever expected. She turned to him with big blue eyes.

And burst into tears.

J J had been only seven when she first discovered the power of tears.

She'd gotten caught by her father sneaking a cookie. Her dad was a stickler for the no-sweets-before-dinner rule. Sneaking a cookie without asking was grounds for losing her television privileges. The moment her eyes had filled with tears, her father had started to shift on his feet. She'd added a sniffle and before she knew it, he was shoving a cookie at her.

She'd learned it applied to men in general when she'd tried it on her first boyfriend at the age of twelve, Sal Morini. Sal had tried to break up with her before the seventh grade dance so he could go out with a girl who'd put out. Namely Vicki Dematto. As soon as she'd turned on the tears, he'd backtracked. Of course at the dance she'd ditched him to party with Lucia and her friends, then told Vicci Dematto what he'd said. No girl had gone out with Sal the rest of the year.

Those early experiences had been eye-opening experiences and led to an epiphany for JJ. Ever since, she'd never had an issue using her big blue eyes to get her out of trouble.

But this time, she wasn't pulling a sympathy card or being manipulative at all. She was honestly just overwhelmed.

And furious that Jonas was the one to witness it.

But, he didn't seem to be enjoying it any more than she was. He stared at her in shock before swinging his eyes back to the road.

"Oh God, I'm sorry. I wasn't trying to yell at you."

Hearing him backtracking somehow only made it worse. She was a strong, independent woman and she didn't need to be pandered to. It was humiliating that she was crying right now when all she wanted to do was rage, but after being so sure that someone was following her, her emotions were raw and right at the surface.

"I'm not crying about that. Damn it, why am I crying at all?" She swiped at her cheeks and glared at him, as if the tears were his fault.

Although maybe they were partially his fault. She'd been holding it together while walking on her own. Then Jonas had to show up looking all kinds of edible and reminding her how much her safety meant to everyone else. Of course she'd broken down! What woman wouldn't, after a guilt trip like that?

Never mind that what he'd said wasn't even that bad. JJ needed someone to blame just then, and Jonas was readily available.

"You show up talking about Lucia and my safety. I thought someone was following me, so I told him I had a Taser and a dick, but really, all I had was the dick and I was scared, because even if that dick is huge, I mean it's probably more effective as a club."

Jonas glanced at her from the corner of his eye, and then mouthed the word *dick* slowly. Under any other circumstances JJ would have laughed. He had the cautious expression you use when talking to someone who is completely batshit crazy.

Maybe she had lost it. She reached back into her purse and pulled it out. "See, I have a legitimate dick."

His eyes went wide. "Damn, I think that thing is setting some unrealistic expectations."

She rolled her eyes. "It's not for me to use, asshole. It was a gag gift that Lucia gave back. And it was all I had as a weapon."

He worked hard to wipe the smirk off his face. "Jessica, I apologize if I made you feel like I was coming down hard on you. I just want you to know that your safety is our top priority."

He made another turn that had her shifting slightly, almost falling into the door. Part of her wanted to give him shit for his driving, but she couldn't even muster the energy. She'd been running on pure adrenaline before, but now that she was tucked into the safe confines of the car with Jonas, the fear from before came back full force. What the hell had that been about? She'd heard something; there was no way she'd imagined that. And if she'd heard something, and someone had been there, why hadn't they answered when she called out? Why would anyone want to scare her?

She ignored the voice in the back of her head. *You know who might.*

No. That was her old life. Things were different now. *Are you sure? Because maybe the fire wasn't an accident.*

She couldn't go down that spiral again. She had a brand new life now.

They pulled into the underground garage in the Blake Security building. JJ had been so deep in her thoughts that she hadn't even realized they were home. *Home.* The place you were supposed to feel safe. JJ hadn't felt like that about any place in a long time. But she could honestly acknowledge that she'd felt like that the past few months living with Lucia and her crew. Her living arrangements had seemed like a gross overreaction to her friend's security issues the prior year, but she'd soon come to love it. Surrounded by muscular, hot men all the time and living rent free. Not a bad deal at all.

But now she could see that she'd allowed it to lull her into a false sense of security. Sure she was safer living with the Blake Security team, but she must never let herself think she was truly safe. No matter where she went, she would never be safe.

"You know you can come to me with anything, right?"

JJ looked over to see that Jonas had cut the car off and turned in his seat so he could watch her. Suddenly self-conscious, she pushed her hair behind her ear.

"Sure. I mean, it's your job."

"No. Not just because it's my job."

Awareness blossomed and JJ flushed. His eyes didn't leave hers. She fidgeted with the strap of her bag, unsure how to handle this side of him. It was weird to have him looking at her like this and being nice to her. Angry and argumentative Jonas? She could handle him with one hand tied behind her back. But tender, sex-on-a-stick Jonas? Well, she didn't have the first clue as to how to act. What if she admitted that she'd wanted to call him earlier? What if she told him that she thought of him when she was alone in her bed at night and he laughed?

She'd die instantly.

"Well, I'm fine," she protested weakly. "I don't need anyone's help."

"Maybe not, but I do."

"You need my help," JJ replied, deliberately misunderstanding him.

She could tell by the flare of heat in his eyes that he was gearing up for one of their knock down, drag out wars of words. Her body responded in kind. For the first time, she catalogued the symptoms like an outsider. Increased heart rate and breathing. Flushed skin and a sense of anticipation.

God. It was so obvious looking back on it now. The whole time they'd been fighting they'd been engaging in foreplay. She could only wonder if it was as obvious to everyone else in the house. Probably. Which was just great. How was she supposed to look the others in the eye now?

"I need you to want my help. I need to help you. Because the idea of anyone fucking with you makes me crazy."

The idea that Jonas would unleash his rage on someone just because they'd bothered her pleased her greatly. She clamped down on the response. It was far too close to a "girlfriend" type of thing, and way too possessive for her taste. She'd had more than enough of possessive men who thought they owned her.

"What did I just say? Something just made the light go out of your eyes."

She shook her head. "Nothing. But I don't want anyone getting hurt because of me. I just want to be left alone."

"Who isn't allowing you to be left alone?"

Damn him for being so smart. The only way to keep from giving him all the clues he needed was to distract him. Luckily, she knew the perfect way to do that.

"Right now the only one annoying me is you. So I guess I'll say thanks for the ride and good night."

Before he could react, she reached over the console and grabbed the front of his shirt. He let her tug him until he was close enough for her to smell the scent of his cologne. Their eyes met, and suddenly Jonas smiled. The impact of it, especially so close, made JJ feel like she was flying. And suddenly this wasn't about distracting him anymore. It was about doing what she'd wanted to do for ages.

Kiss him.

His lips softened under hers and he let out a soft groan that ricocheted through the still interior of the car. It was incredibly intimate, secluded there with just the two of them and the rapidly increasing sound of their breathing.

For those moments, they weren't Jonas and JJ, mortal enemies.

They were two people who connected like lightning, taking each other in like they wanted to merge into one being.

She gasped and a moan slipped loose. Jonas took that opportunity to slip his hand into her hair, anchor her head, and deepen the kiss, his tongue sliding over hers expertly.

JJ hooked her arm around his neck, holding him still, and he opened his mouth wider like he was trying to swallow her whole. If the console hadn't been between them, she likely would have climbed into his lap, but instead she just sucked on his lower lip until he moaned into her mouth, the sound finally bringing her back to reality.

They stayed for a beat staring at each other before she pulled back and opened the door. The rush of cool air coming in cleared her head, and JJ wondered if it had finally happened. After years of pretending to be okay, if maybe she'd finally had a mental breakdown.

"JJ, what just—"

"Good night, Jonas." She closed the door and walked quickly to the elevator.

For the first time that day, luck was on her side, because after she leaned forward for the retinal scan, the doors opened immediately.

The doors closed just as Jonas rushed up. She heard his muffled curse get fainter as the elevator ascended.

"Good night, indeed." JJ touched her mouth.

One-click the next book, Force!

Also available at www.malonesquared.com/force

ABOUT THE AUTHORS

M. MALONE is a 2019 RITA® Award winner and a NYT & USA Today Bestselling author of completely inappropriate romantic comedy. She lives in Northern Virginia with her three favorite guys, her husband and their two sons. She holds a Master's degree in Business from a prestigious college that would no doubt be scandalized by how she's using her expensive education. She's now a full-time writer and spends 99.8% of her time in her pajamas. minxmalone.com

USA Today Bestselling Author, **NANA MALONE**'s love of all things romance started when she was thirteen with a book she borrowed from her cousin on a sultry summer afternoon in Ghana.

Waiting for her chance at a job as a ninja assassin, Nana, meantime works out her drama, passion and sass with fictional characters every bit as sassy and kick butt as she thinks she is. nanamaloneromance.net

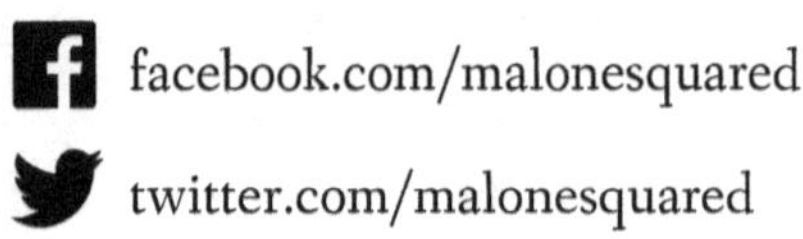

facebook.com/malonesquared

twitter.com/malonesquared